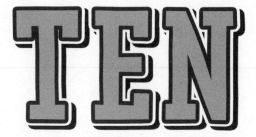

TEN

A Soccer Story

Shamini Flint

Clarion Books
Houghton Mifflin Harcourt
Boston New York

Clarion Books

3 Park Avenue

New York, New York 10016

Copyright © 2009 by Shamini Flint

This edition published in 2015 by Allen & Unwin

First published in Singapore in 2009 by Sunbear Publishing Pte. Ltd.

Clarion Books is an imprint of Houghton Mifflin Harcourt Publishing Company.

www.hmhco.com

The text was set in Dante MT.

Design by Lisa Vega

Library of Congress Cataloging-in-Publication Data

Names: Flint, Shamini, 1969– author.

Title: Ten : a soccer story / Shamini Flint.

Description: Boston ; New York : Clarion Books, Houghton Mifflin Harcourt, [2017] |
"First published in Singapore in 2009 by Sunbear Publishing Pte. Ltd."—Copyright page.
| Summary: In 1986 Malaysia, as she worries about her parents' constant fighting, ardent
soccer fan Maya, age eleven, trains herself and pulls together a team at her girls' school,
despite soccer being a "boys' game."

Identifiers: LCCN 2016016164 | ISBN 9780544850019 (hardback)

Subjects: | CYAC: Soccer—Fiction | Sex role—Fiction . | Divorce—Fiction. | Racially
mixed people—Fiction | Malaysia—History—20th century—Fiction | BISAC: JUVENILE
FICTION / Sports & Recreation / Soccer. | JUVENILE FICTION / Girls & Women. |
JUVENILE FICTION / People & Places / Asia. | JUVENILE FICTION / Humorous Stories.
| JUVENILE FICTION / Social Issues / Prejudice & Racism.

Classification: LCC PZ7.F6343 Te 2017 | DDC [Fic]—dc23

LC record available at https://lccn.loc.gov/2016016164

Manufactured in the United States of America

DOC 10 9 8 7 6 5 4 3 2 1

4500655078

For Aryssa—make me proud!

And for my Friday football big boys—Seb, Magnus, Chris,

and Ryan—thanks for letting me play.

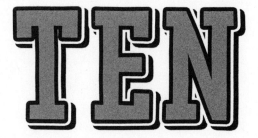

TEN

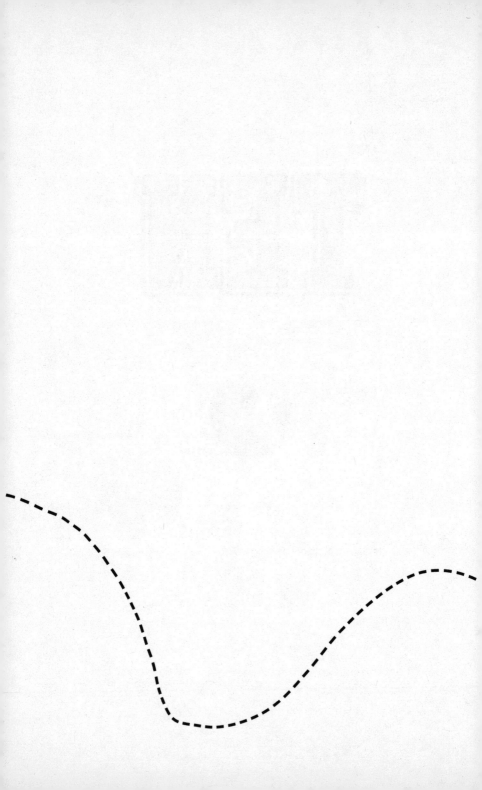

Some people believe soccer is a matter of life and death.

I am very disappointed with that attitude.

I can assure you it is much, much more important than that.

—Bill Shankly, soccer player and manager of the
Liverpool Football Club from 1959 to 1964

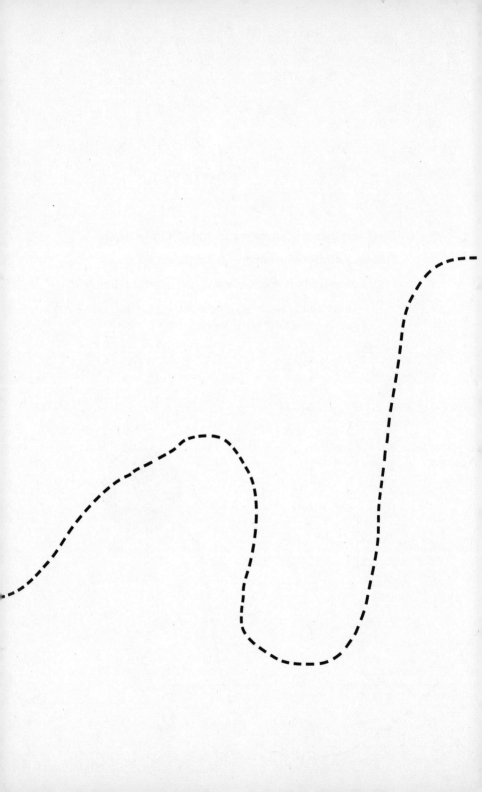

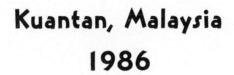

Kuantan, Malaysia
1986

CHAPTER
ONE

The score is 1–1.

They have to send me in. They have no choice. I know it and they know it.

Sure enough, I get the signal from the bench.

My heart is thumping. Games don't come bigger than this —the World Cup quarterfinal between Brazil and France in Mexico.

I *know* we can win this match. But I also know there isn't much time left.

I try to shut out the crowd, to concentrate, to breathe calmly. But it is difficult. The noise is unimaginable. Waves of sound buffet me. Half the stadium is in blue, the other half— my half, the Brazilian half—is in yellow.

My heart swells. I am so proud.

The lineman holds up the board.

My number is chalked on it: 10.

The referee waves me in.

I have a moment of doubt. The newspapers have not been kind. They say I am too old, too fat. What if they're right?

There's only one way to find out. I jog onto the field.

The yellow half goes berserk. Forget the papers. The fans still believe in me. I can hear the hope in their voices and in the frenzied samba beat.

I jog into space. Do a few jinking runs. I feel good. Fit.

Almost immediately I sense the rhythm of the game. Ebb and flow, stop and start. A quick dash, a pass, a feint, and then a flick. My teammates are a talented bunch. I am proud to be on the field with them. The yellow jerseys, the blue shorts, and the white socks. It's magic!

I catch the eye of Sócrates. I see a drop of sweat hanging off his beard. I smile at him. He is *such* a poser. Imagine a professional soccer player with a thick beard and a philosopher's name!

There isn't much time left and the score is still 1–1. But I am so happy to be here.

I pick up the ball in my own half. Dip my shoulder and go around the Frenchman in front of me. Another is rushing in. I let him get in close. Too close. He is committed to a tackle. A quick sidestep and he is left behind. I look up—just a glance —and see a yellow streak racing down the field.

Branco is making a run.

I slide the ball through the middle of the field. The pass is inch-perfect.

Branco picks it up. He is in space. No one to beat but the goalie.

He keeps his head, waltzes into the box and around the goalie — and is brought down!

We turn to the referee. There was no contact with the ball. It must be a . . .

Penalty!!

The referee has given it. I can't believe it. Our luck is turning. This is going to be our day. I can feel it.

All over the pitch, players in yellow jerseys are hugging each other. I see teammates pounce on Branco, who has yet to get up from where he fell.

All eyes turn to me and I remember that I, Zico, am the penalty taker. As I walk slowly forward, I debate my shot.

Right? Left? Straight?

It is important to have a plan. It is even more important not to let the goalie guess my plan.

I adjust the ball on the spot. I take my time. I know that the French goalie, Joël Bats, is more nervous than I am. He can hear the samba. He can see the Brazilians screaming my name out of the corner of his eye. The French fans, his fans, have gone quiet.

I turn around and walk away. I spin back. Take a short run up. I am going right, low and hard. That is my plan.

I see from his body that the goalie is going to his left.

I consider changing my mind.

I don't.

It is not a clean shot.

Bats gets a hand to it. He keeps it out.

There is a stunned silence. Then an uproar from the French crowd. They are chanting *"Vive les Bleus!"* (Long Live the Blues!).

CHAPTER
TWO

I tuck my blanket around me and drag myself back to the living room. No soccer, no cleats, and no screaming fans — except on television.

I am not Zico anymore. I am Maya. I am eleven years old and I've never actually kicked a soccerball. Not a real one. Not even once.

I can hardly believe it. I've pictured myself on the field in hundreds of games. I'm a *brilliant* player, in my head. Usually I imagine I'm Zico, the best soccer player in the world — ever!

It seems so real, being out there in the sunshine with the Brazilians.

It is this dark living room, the cane furniture, the whirring fan, and being all alone in the middle of the night watching the World Cup on television that seem like a dream.

I pinch myself really hard. That's what the kids in books

do to see if they're awake. Ouch! I'm awake, all right. Zico has missed a penalty and now my arm hurts where I pinched it.

I can't believe it. My hero has missed a penalty in the last twenty minutes of a World Cup quarterfinal. A penalty that would have put Brazil in the lead. Probably into the semifinals for a match against the Germans, who are rubbish this year.

Zico's face is close-up on the flickering screen. He looks bewildered—maybe he's wondering if he's dreaming. Probably he wishes he was in a living room somewhere watching the game on television.

He looks chubbier than in the poster I have of him in my bedroom. In my poster he is fit and slim, wearing his socks around his ankles—the "I'm too tough for shin guards" look.

I make excuses for my hero. He'd just come in. He wasn't warmed up yet. They shouldn't have let him take the kick.

It was his pass that led to the goalie fouling Branco—in a way, it was his penalty to miss.

I make excuses for my hero, but I know that Brazil is in deep trouble now.

razil is my favorite soccer team in the whole wide world, but I'm not Brazilian.

I'm Malaysian, and I live in a small coastal town called Kuantan with my mom and dad and my brother, Rajiv, who is older than me and a real pain.

Once every four years, during the World Cup, I support Brazil. More than that, I feel Brazilian. That's because of the way the team plays soccer. It might be the World Cup, but they play like kids on a beach. Besides, Malaysia never qualifies for the World Cup—and I have to support *someone*.

The match is almost over. Still 1–1.

The sounds from upstairs are getting louder. It's Mom and Dad, of course. They're not interested in soccer. It's three in the morning. But they're awake.

And they're yelling.

I don't know what they're yelling about. I can't make out the words. That doesn't matter, really. What it's about makes no difference. I used to believe that if we could all sit down and talk about whatever was wrong, we could fix it. Now I know better. My parents fight because they have forgotten how to stop.

I stuff my fingers in my ears. I can still hear them. I just hate how angry they sound. Dad is gruff—I'd be afraid of him if I didn't know he was my dad. Mom is crying. I can always tell—I don't have to be in the room to see tears. Shouting while crying makes your voice funny, sort of like playing soccer with a bad cold and then having to stop and yell at the referee because he's just given you a yellow card for faking an injury.

Mom and Dad try to save up their arguments until Rajiv and I are in bed. I guess they hope we won't realize what they're doing.

When we were younger, Rajiv and I would rush upstairs and try to break up their fights. Rajiv was like the referee of a game where the players start shoving each other—he'd get between them. I'd be like one of the senior players and try to drag one of them away.

Then we'd both beg them to stop and cry hot tears of our own.

Sometimes it worked.

Mostly they'd tell us to go back to bed and not to worry because it was a grown-up problem and not about us children, and we shouldn't worry about things we were too young to understand.

Sometimes, instead of rushing up, I'd climb into bed with Rajiv and we'd both lie awake and listen to the yelling.

"Do you think they'll get a divorce?" I asked him once.

"What? Of course not!"

"How can you be so sure?"

"Do you know anyone in the history of mankind who's gotten a *divorce* in this town?"

"No."

"See?" He was triumphant.

"Maybe the other parents don't argue," I pointed out.

"Some of them must, surely."

I thought of all the couples I knew, parents of schoolmates and the hordes of relatives on Mom's side. It was hard to believe that they were all perfectly happy; there were some real nutjobs in the mix.

"Anyway, just because they don't always get along doesn't mean they're getting a divorce," insisted Rajiv.

I decided to take his word for it. He's older than I am. I guess he knows more about this sort of stuff. I hoped so, anyway. I couldn't bear to imagine not living with Mom or Dad or even Rajiv.

Nowadays when they fight we just pretend it's not happening.

I turn up the volume on the TV. It's much easier to pretend it's not happening if I can't hear them.

The referee blows his whistle. The full-time score between Brazil and France is 1–1.

This World Cup quarterfinal game will be decided on penalties.

Sócrates takes the first kick.

He walks up. I know what he is going to do. In that second, watching him, I know he is going for placement, not power.

I just pray he doesn't pick the same spot, top left corner, the way he did in the last game. The goalie will be waiting for that.

Sócrates picks the same spot. Top left corner. The goalie is waiting for it.

Joël Bats keeps it out with a fine acrobatic save.

Zico steps forward.

I feel as if my heart might burst. How brave he is to agree to take another spot kick so soon after missing the last one. What if he misses again? He might be brave, but he must also be stupid to take such a risk. Maybe Dad is right when he says soccer players carry their brains in their shoes. No one will ever forget the man who missed *two* penalties in a World Cup knockout game. They'll probably note it on his tombstone: RIP ZICO: TOOK TWO, MISSED TWO.

I cover my face with my hands. I can't bear to watch.

But I peek through the cracks between my fingers. I have to watch.

I go limp with fear.

Zico scores.

Maybe this will turn out all right in the end!

Platini misses—he gets under the ball and it flies over the crossbar.

Maybe this could really, really turn out all right . . .

Júlio César hits the post.

Luis Fernández converts for France, and Brazil is out of the World Cup. Again.

Zico—they call him the White Pelé—will never win a World Cup medal now.

I switch off the TV and sit quietly in the darkness. There is silence upstairs as well. Mom and Dad have gone to bed.

T hat Zico is just useless," crows my brother.

I stay silent. I knew breakfast would be tough.

Mom flips a dosa, a sort of Indian pancake, off the flat, metal skillet and onto my plate. As if I could eat anything after last night.

She says to Rajiv, "Don't pick on your sister. You know she takes her soccer seriously."

My brother ignores her. "He missed a penalty! How could he miss a penalty?"

I wonder how he knows. The useless sod didn't even watch the game. He must have heard about it from a friend.

Rajiv slaps some peanut butter onto a slice of bread and shoves the whole thing into his mouth. He doesn't like Indian food, so he won't eat the dosa Mom is cooking. His mouth is gummed shut with the sticky stuff and he can't speak for a moment.

I'm glad. I need a break from his teasing. I don't think it's funny.

Mom is upset that I'm not eating. She is staring at my untouched food with that worried expression she gets if she feels she isn't feeding us kids enough.

Rajiv and I usually eat as though we've played ninety minutes of soccer just before breakfast, but we're still tall and skinny. Our relatives are always telling Mom to put some meat on our bones, especially mine. Today I have no appetite. After all, Brazil just got eliminated from the World Cup.

My grandmother totters in. She is wearing a white sari. I have not seen her wear anything else since Granddad died five years ago. Mom says it is a sign that Amamma (that's what we call her) is still in mourning and that she is not long for this world. Dad doesn't say it out loud, but I know he thinks it's been quite long enough, thanks very much.

I wouldn't rush to catch up with Granddad in that great soccer field in the sky if I were Amamma. He was a nasty piece of work. My clearest memory is of him lying in an armchair and trying to hit his grandkids with his walking stick if they wandered too close.

The walking stick had an ivory handle carved to look like the head of a rhinoceros hornbill. I remember the cane so clearly because my grandfather had a huge beak for a nose. Sideways, he looked a lot like his cane.

Amamma does not always live with us. She rotates among her three children, my two uncles and my mother.

But when she is here, the shouting upstairs gets louder.

Now she says, "You need to feed the children better. Look at Maya. All skin and bones. No one will marry her."

I'm eleven and she's already worried that no one will marry me. I'm not concerned. If I can't actually *be* Zico, I plan to marry Zico.

Mom is defending me. "Of course someone will marry her!" she says indignantly.

What is it with these people?

I feel like shouting, "Hello, I'm only *eleven*."

I must have yelled it out loud because there is a sudden silence. My brother manages to mutter through the peanut butter, "Never too early to start worrying, if you ask me." He chortles.

He's a fine one to talk. It's pretty clear he's inherited Granddad's nose.

Amamma ignores my brother and me and continues goading Mom. She pulls out her trump card. "No one would marry *you*," she points out to Mom, cackling and showing off the few teeth sprouting on her red gums like dirty brown mushrooms.

"Dad married Mom," I exclaim indignantly, forgetting for a moment that it isn't exactly a match made in heaven, what with the yelling every night.

"That doesn't count. No *Indian* man would marry your mother. That is why she had to marry a white man."

It is impossible to reason with Amamma, but I try anyway.

I always thought I would be really good at talking to those people who stand on bridges threatening to jump — I am sure I could persuade them not to. I have a lot of patience. You need it in my family.

I say firmly, "There is nothing wrong with marrying someone different."

"Pah! If there's nothing wrong, then why all the screaming and shouting every night? Worse than a hen house. Nobody cares that an old woman needs her sleep."

At least she didn't say beauty sleep.

I look at Mom and Rajiv, hoping one of them will come in like a last-minute substitute and score the winning goal, but they're happy warming the bench.

"It's quite normal to disagree once in a while. I bet you fought with Granddad sometimes."

"Never! I knew my proper place in a marriage."

Out of reach of the walking stick, I almost said but didn't. For all I know, Amamma inherited that stick and it's waiting in a closet somewhere.

"If Mom hadn't married Dad, we wouldn't be here."

A winning argument, surely? What grandmother would argue against the existence of her own grandchildren?

Mine, apparently.

"Now you and your brother are half-breeds. You belong nowhere."

"I suppose you think it would be better if Mom and Dad got a divorce?" The missed penalty had made me reckless.

Amamma turned gray, which is what happens when dark-skinned people grow pale.

"Of course they're not getting a divorce."

"How do you know?"

"It's not our way."

"Our way?"

"Asians, Indians, Malaysians—marriage is forever. Except for some in the big city who think they're very modern."

"But Dad is white. I bet people get divorced all the time in England."

"Even your father would not dare do that to me. I wouldn't know where to hide my face."

I considered making a few suggestions and then thought better of it.

"If your mother had been fair-skinned with a bit of flesh on her bones, some nice Indian boy from a good family would have married her, and this whole thing would not have happened. You'd better eat."

I roll my eyes at Mom. She is smiling at me, but her mouth is twisted down at the corners, so I know it is one of those smiles that mean she is proud of me but unhappy inside. I recognize it

because I have the same sort of smile sometimes. I do my best
—I bend my lips upward the way you're supposed to, but then
my heart hurts and the corners of my mouth turn down suddenly. I smile back at Mom. It is a twisty smile too and a mirror
of hers.

Mom is short and plump (although not, according to
Amamma, when she was younger and looking for an Indian
husband) and has fluffy, wispy hair. She looks like a mother—
overweight enough to be cuddly, messy in a frazzled sort of way,
and always with a worried look on her face as if she's trying to
remember whether she turned off the gas after cooking or fed
the neighbors' cat for them.

She wears only friendly colors like light pink and light blue.
Her hair is windblown even on days when there is no wind,
because she runs her fingers through it when she is exasperated.

Now she runs her fingers through her hair and decides
belatedly to argue with Amamma. She really should know by
now that there is never overtime in matches with Amamma.

She says, "Well, they may be thin, but they are fair! Why
should you be worried?"

Amamma always has the last word on any subject. She spits,
"They are not fair, they are *white!*"

She makes it sound like a nasty skin condition—scabies or
eczema.

Mom doesn't insist that she and Dad will never get a divorce, even if it's just to avoid embarrassing Amamma. I try to put the thought out of my mind, but it lurks there like a striker in the box.

Rajiv finally swallows his peanut butter sandwich. I wonder for a split second if he is going to quarrel with Amamma. But Rajiv knows better. He doesn't pick fights unless he knows he can win.

That's why he picks them with me.

"I bet I'd have scored that penalty," he says.

This is too much.

"You don't even play soccer," I sneer.

That annoys him. I know, because when he is annoyed his nose turns white around the nostrils and the tip glows pink.

"Neither do you! Anyway, I don't play soccer because I *choose* not to play soccer. I prefer hockey."

"Stupid game," I mutter. "Who needs a stick if you have feet?"

"Not as stupid as soccer. Especially the way Brazilians play it. Last time it was the semis, this time the quarters—next time they probably won't even qualify. What are you going to do then?"

It's true what he says. I remember all too clearly. Italy's hat trick, scored by that nobody, Paolo Rossi, against Brazil in the semifinal of the last World Cup. That time it was defensive weakness that cost us—Brazil, I mean—the game. This time we were just wretched at penalties. Who could have imagined that Sócrates and Zico would both miss penalties? Platini too. But his miss will be forgotten because it didn't cost France the game.

"Your Zico will never win a World Cup now!"

I look at Rajiv numbly. Zico, the best player at this World Cup and the last, will never win a World Cup. The dream is over. Even if I manage to marry him, the poor fellow will be a train wreck.

Rajiv knows he has really upset me. His nose turns entirely white. This indicates regret. He would never admit it, but I know how to read that nose.

Amamma says, "I don't know why all those grown men are chasing one ball. Why doesn't someone buy them one each?"

Mom is so short that she can't see over the steering wheel when she drives us to school. We have an old square, silver Volvo, which Mom says will do very well for her coffin someday. I think she is joking, but I can't be sure. She peers through the gap between the steering wheel rim and the middle bit with the horn. She swerves as a motor scooter appears out of nowhere. For her, that is. I saw the silly fellow with his unbuckled helmet coming up on the inside lane ages ago. I am eleven and I am already taller than she is.

"Mom!"

"Sorry, honey. I didn't see him."

She hunches forward and retracts her neck slightly like a fearful tortoise.

Rajiv says, "You should just let me drive, Mom."

"Don't be silly, Rajiv. You're far too young. It will be years before you get your license."

I am with Rajiv on this. He is very good at mechanical things. He can use power tools and hang pictures and fix the washing machine. He may be too young to drive, but there is no doubt in my mind he would do a better job than Mom. At least he would be able to see the road.

Mom swerves again. Maybe she's right and this Volvo *is* going to be our coffin.

She almost takes out an entire family on a scooter, the father wearing his jacket back to front, the mother with one arm around his waist and the other clutching a baby to her side; a toddler is standing on the platform of the little Vespa, penned in by her father's outstretched hands. Only the parents are wearing helmets. The little girl's hair is streaming behind her in the wind. She's having fun.

Mom mutters something about irresponsible parents. It's true that what they are doing is unsafe, but I feel sorry for them. The dad must be a fisherman from one of the villages farther up the coast. It's monsoon season now, when the seas are too rough to go out fishing. The fishermen don't make much money at this time of year. There's no way he could afford a car. And there are hardly any buses. Besides, the buses are almost as dangerous as the motor scooters—hurtling down the narrow, windy streets, jam-packed with so many passengers that there isn't even standing room and the conductor has to lean out the door.

The only other transport is by rickshaw. But pedal power

has never been the quickest way of getting about. I'm not sure that whole family could get into a rickshaw anyway. And if they did, they might be too heavy for the rickshaw driver. Usually, rickshaws are powered by the oldest people you ever saw, with wrinkly skin and lucky moles sprouting tufts of hair on their chins.

Mom drops Rajiv off first, and then we go farther into town to my school. Our schools were originally Catholic missions; mine is a girls' school and Rajiv's has only boys.

I desperately wish there were boys at my school too. It's not that I like boys or anything, even Rajiv. I'm not like those girls, especially in some of the older classes, who spend all their time talking about boys and which ones are *so* cute.

I wish there were boys in school because if there were boys, there would be soccer. Rajiv has soccer coaching and he says the other boys' schools have it too. I'd put up with the boys for the soccer.

Did I mention that I have never, ever kicked a soccerball (except in my head)? I can *imagine* myself dribbling past defenders and doing step overs and back heels. But I can't play in real life. That's because my school teaches the girls to play only netball and field hockey.

Netball! Easily the dumbest game ever invented; probably the dumbest *anything* ever invented. I don't even like basketball, which is quite like netball and almost as dreadful. In netball, when you get the ball, you stop running. How stupid is that?

And, depending on which position you play, you're not allowed to leave certain parts of the court. There are lines you're not supposed to cross. Can you imagine? You're running into position, someone passes you the ball, and you stop. Or you're running and you reach some line on the field and you stop.

I play netball very badly. And I'm not ashamed of it. It would be an embarrassment to be good at something so ridiculous.

Mom has gotten me to the school gates without hitting anything. I get out and wave goodbye quickly. I'm late because of the argument with Amamma over breakfast.

The first class is English. Sister Pauline doesn't like anyone to be late. I walk through the big swinging doors into the airy classroom. Sister Pauline is standing at the front, wielding a piece of chalk like a light saber. She is a nun and is wearing her habit. Dad calls it dressing like a penguin. Mom says Dad should have more respect for religion.

Sister Pauline tells Sok Mun, "God loves homework."

Sok Mun's mom died when she was born and her dad has a stall at the market where he sells cut-up fruit. She helps out every day, so sometimes she's too tired or doesn't have time to do her homework. Dad says it's child labor and he has a good mind to report it. He's been saying that for two years now, but he hasn't done it. I guess he knows that Sok Mun's dad asks for her help because he really needs it. You don't make much money selling cut fruit. (I know this because Mom usually buys from him when we go to the market.) He works at the stall for really long hours. If Sok Mun and the rest of his kids didn't take turns helping him, the family probably wouldn't have enough to eat.

If I'm on time for school, I let Sok Mun copy my homework. Today I'm too late.

I am still useful to her, though—as a distraction. Sister Pauline forgets about her and turns to me.

She says, "God loves punctuality, Maya."

I've noticed that God always seems to love whatever it is that a pupil has failed to do or be.

I say, "Yes, Sister Pauline," in my most docile voice, the one Rajiv says makes him want to puke and would dissuade the fiercest referee from handing out a red card—even for a blatant handball in the penalty box.

It works.

Sister Pauline says, "Well, don't do it again," but doesn't make me stand on the chair or on the table or in the corner or hold my ears and do squats or write lines on the blackboard about what God loves (Sister Pauline must believe that God loves lines).

CHAPTER
SIX

nother girl walks in late and my heart sinks.

It is Batumalar.

I've barely had a good day at school since she joined the class a few weeks ago.

"Late again, Batumalar?" asks Sister Pauline.

Batumalar murmurs something—maybe it's an excuse or an explanation—but I can't hear what it is. It wouldn't matter anyway.

"In the corner. I want fifty squats."

The whole class gasps. That's the most any girl has ever had to do.

"That will teach Batumalar not to be *Batu Malas*," says Sister Pauline, and there are titters from the class.

It's really not funny. "Batu Malas" means "Lazy Stone" in Malay. We do all our schoolwork, except English, in the Malay language. This is hard, because not all the kids speak Malay when they start school—I didn't. It took me ages to understand what was going on.

Batumalar walks to the corner. She crosses her hands so that she is holding opposite ears and starts squatting and standing, squatting and standing. Batumalar is square and strong and looks like she's been hewn from rock. Watching her strained face now is to understand how earthquakes happen.

Some of the girls look away and others stare.

I don't know which is worse. To look would make her shame worse. I'd bet my collection of Beverly Cleary books that Zico wished the stadium was empty when he missed that penalty. But to look away is to abandon her. Maybe Zico would have felt better if he had known that in a small town in Malaysia, an eleven-year-old girl was making excuses for his penalty miss.

Batumalar is the only other Indian in the class. Most people in Malaysia are Malays and Chinese, but there are a few Indians too.

Mom is from one of the oldest Indian families in the area. Just about all the other Indians in town are our relatives, while plantation Indians like Batumalar and her family are not. An aunt of mine was even head girl of my school a few years back.

Dad being white annoys Amamma because she is very particular about bloodlines. But the kids in school think it's cool. That's because they don't know any white people in real life. They assume they must all be like Superman or Batman, which, if you knew my dad, you would realize was really funny. His tummy hangs over his trousers, he wears thick glasses, and he chews on a toothpick all the time.

Batumalar is an Indian from one of the estates—the rubber plantations—outside town. Her dad taps rubber. That's what you call it when your job is to cut a thin strip of bark off each rubber tree and collect the sap that drips into a cup.

For some reason he has sent his daughter, Batumalar, to this convent school. Most of the plantation children go to the Tamil school on the estate. Tamil is the language that a lot of Indians in Malaysia speak, including Mom.

I do too, just a little, but we speak English at home. Otherwise Dad wouldn't have a clue as to what we were talking about.

I asked Mom why Batumalar doesn't go to the estate school. She said maybe Batumalar's dad wants something better for his daughter. The school I go to is considered pretty good, even if it does have Sister Pauline.

Batumalar is often late because her dad has to bring her all the way from the estate on his scooter every morning. She said to me once that it took an hour and fifteen minutes each way.

I wonder whether she has ever told her dad that she gets bullied at school, even by some teachers. That they call her Batu Malas and make her do more squats than anyone else.

I guess not.

Her dad would have taken her out of the school if he knew. I was sure of that. Probably she didn't want him to be disappointed that all his effort of getting her into a good school was for nothing.

CHAPTER
SEVEN

I know it's tough to be a minority (like Batumalar and me) because when I was six years old, my Dad told me so. I had kind of guessed by then too.

Dad was working on a project for the VSO at the time, which is like the Peace Corps but for English people. Folks come out to other countries to help them with stuff—such as teaching English in schools and building drains.

I was sent to a village school in that area.

On my first day of school *ever*, I was really excited.

By the third class I was in terrible trouble.

Puan Sharifah, my teacher, told me to sit in an empty classroom. By myself.

I sat there for ages wondering what I had done wrong.

I was too embarrassed to tell Mom that I'd been punished on my first day of school. Besides, she was bound to ask me what I had done wrong, and I hadn't a clue.

On the second day of school, I was sent to the empty classroom again. I was really upset this time. I'd been as quiet as a mouse to avoid doing whatever it was that got me punished the first day.

I sat there for a while in the big empty classroom, and then I decided that school was not for me.

So I sneaked out and walked home.

It was a three-kilometer walk. I was six years old. Mom says that to this day, nothing has ever given her as much of a shock as seeing me stumble through the front gate, sobbing. I wouldn't normally have cried, but I'd been walking for ages, my feet hurt, and the whole way I'd been wondering what I could have done that was so bad I had to be sent out of the room two days in a row.

I swear that when I walked in, for a moment Mom was as white as Dad.

Mom took me back to school, of course.

She was really upset that I'd been punished and that nobody had even bothered to tell me what I'd done wrong. Also, that I'd walked all the way home and could have gotten lost or run over or kidnapped.

When we went back to school, a whole bunch of teachers were standing by the gates looking worried. Puan Sharifah hugged me and burst into tears, and then everyone apologized at once.

Mom asked, "But why did you punish Maya?"

"Punish her?" Puan Sharifah looked puzzled. She still had her arm around my shoulders.

"Yes, and on the first two days of school!"

"But I didn't punish her."

I pulled away from her and yelled, "Yes, you did! You sent me out of class. Yesterday and today. And I didn't do anything. *Really* I didn't."

The teacher stared at me as if I'd gone mad.

Then she started to laugh and Mom and I stared at her as if *she*'d gone mad.

Mom said in her stiffest imitation of a white person's voice, which she'd picked up from Dad, "This is no laughing matter."

Puan Sharifah wiped her eyes and said, "You are right. But she was not punished. She was asked to wait in another class because it was the Islamic Studies lesson and she is the *only* non-Muslim in the class."

Mom was trying to stay angry. She said, "You should have explained."

The teacher nodded. She turned to me and said, "I'm sorry, Maya. You're the only Indian *and* the only non-Muslim in the class, you see."

I didn't see. Not until bedtime that night, when Mom explained that there were so many religions in Malaysia, kids were taught only their own so as not to offend anyone. It just so happened that at my new school all the kids were Malay Muslims—except me.

"But what religion are we, Mom?"

Mom said, "Well, I was brought up a Hindu."

And Dad said, "I have no time for this religious nonsense."

"But why didn't they have a class for me about being a Hindu or something?"

Dad said, "Not enough kids in the class for them to pay a teacher. You were in a minority of one."

Now I'm in a minority of two.

Me and Batumalar.

The only two Indians in the class, and one of us is getting picked on and the other is too terrified of being picked on to do anything about it.

"You were right, Dad."

"About what?"

"It's tough being a minority."

CHAPTER
EIGHT

've decided I'm going to be a professional soccer player when I grow up.

I feel the hand of God on my shoulder.

All right; I don't really.

But Diego Maradona has just scored two goals that I'll never forget in Argentina's World Cup quarterfinal against England. He is an *amazing* player. Not as good as Zico, of course. Actually, the truth is he might be better, but I'll never admit that to anyone.

Maradona is short and stocky and cries a lot. Dad says all South Americans are like that.

For the first goal, he jumps with Peter Shilton and manages to get the ball over Shilton's head and into the net.

Peter Shilton must be the best goalie in the tournament.

"How did a runt like Maradona beat him in the air?" Dad wants to know.

The replays make it clear—Maradona used his hand but the referee didn't see the foul. He cheated!

Much later, after the match, Maradona explains that he scored "a bit with the head of Maradona and another bit with the hand of God."

Dad, who is watching the game with me because England is playing, even though he knows nothing about soccer, is furious.

"Scoundrel!" he shouts.

Mom, who is watching the game with me because England is playing, even though she knows nothing about soccer, is delighted.

Dad says Mom has a chip on her shoulder about the English because Malaysia was a British colony (that means Britain ruled most of it) for so long. I think Mom just likes annoying Dad.

For the second goal, Maradona doesn't need God.

He wins the ball in his own half, jinks past five English players, and scores low past Shilton.

I've never seen anything like it.

Dad falls silent.

Mom bounces up and down. She says, "It's Argentina's turn to win!"

Later, she explains that Britain went to war with Argentina to steal back a couple of small islands called the Falklands, which the British insisted belonged to them, even though the islands were right next to Argentina. (Dad says that everyone on the Falklands was British and wanted to stay that way.)

Maybe Maradona was right. Perhaps it was the hand of God. Maybe God was giving Argentinians their revenge because they had been bullied by the British.

I doubt it, though.

Sister Pauline made Batumalar stand in the corner of the classroom for the entire school day today. God didn't step in to help her just because she was being bullied.

CHAPTER
NINE

I f I'm going to be a professional soccer player, I need ball skills. And the only way to get ball skills is to practice.

First, I need a ball.

I know that in Brazil, a lot of children from poor families start playing on the streets using rolled-up wads of newspaper. I would do that but I'm already eleven, so there is no time to waste.

I decide that it will be much better for my career to skip the newspaper-ball bit and progress straight to a real ball. Unfortunately, this means my career choice cannot remain a secret.

It's dinnertime, and we are having rice, fried fish, chicken curry, and beans. We are sitting together at the glass-topped dining table. Rajiv and I would much rather eat in front of the television, but my dad is quite old-fashioned about that.

There hasn't been much conversation. Whatever Mom and Dad were fighting about last night after the soccer game is not over. It never is, really. There are just different stages in the argument. Right now we're post-match. That means they're too tired to keep fighting, but they can't talk about anything else because they're still angry, so they just eat in a grumpy silence.

A good time to introduce a new subject, I think.

"Mom, Dad, may I have a soccerball?"

Rajiv looks up with interest. "Why do you want a soccerball?"

"Why do you think? To play soccer, of course."

"But you can't play."

"Yes, I can."

"No, you can't."

We go on like this for a while until Mom puts up her hand —our signal to stop.

"Why *do* you want a soccerball, Maya?"

"To play!" I am getting impatient. Why else would I want a soccerball?

"Are you sure? I know you love to watch soccer, but you haven't really played, have you?"

"That's because I haven't got a ball," I explain in my best "this is your last warning—next time I'm sending you off" referee's voice.

"You've never asked for one before," says Dad.

"It will keep my nose out of a book," I point out.

My parents are always complaining that I have my nose in a book and that talking to me is like talking to a wall.

Amamma wades in. "Why do you want to play soccer?"

Mom leaps to my defense. "She just wants to have some fun."

I'm not having any of that.

"I'm going to be a professional soccer player," I say firmly.

Amamma shudders. "I can't believe you're my grand-daughter! But why should I be surprised? I can't believe your mother is my daughter."

I am about to respond when I see the vein in Dad's neck writhing like a snake that's been hit on the head with a shovel. I shut my mouth. It's good practice for when I'm a professional soccer player and I've already been shown a yellow card. Knowing when to be quiet is a sure way of not seeing red on the field.

"Girls can't play soccer," interrupts Rajiv.

I kick him under the table.

He falls off the chair, clutching his leg and yelling, the big whiner. I didn't kick him that hard.

Mom grins suddenly. "Well, Rajiv. She's got a good kick on her. I think she *should* have a soccerball."

Dad starts to laugh. Mom does too. Rajiv stops yelling.

For a moment, we feel like a family at the dinner table. It's almost better than Mom agreeing to get me the ball.

This is one of the weirdest things about Mom and Dad. They fight all the time. But sometimes we can all laugh together.

If they really hate each other that much, how come they can do that?

If they don't really hate each other, then why do they have to fight?

That night in bed, I make myself a training program of all the skills I need to master—dribbling, passing (who will I pass to? I put a question mark next to "passing"), shooting, back heels, and step overs.

There's probably more I need to know.

What do you call it when Zico drags the ball onto his foot with his back to the goal, flicks it into the air over his own head, spins around on the spot, and volleys the ball into the top corner of the goal?

I chew the end of my pencil and add "other skills" to the list. I can't describe every single magical thing Zico can do with a soccerball or I'd never get around to practicing.

CHAPTER
TEN

The next day is Saturday, which is good because we always go to the beach in the morning for a picnic. Mom packs nasi lemak, or rice cooked with pandan leaves (smells like vanilla ice cream), anchovy paste with ground dried chilies in it, sliced cucumber, and lots of water because this stuff can blow your head off, it's that spicy.

Rajiv and I jump into the car in our bathing suits so we don't have to waste time changing. At the last moment, Amamma decides to come along, which spoils everyone's mood for a while, but there are great stretches of open sand, so we should be able to stay away from her.

"If I had my soccerball, I could practice on the beach, Mom."

"Be patient, Maya," says Mom. Amamma just scowls.

The sea is as beautiful as ever—green, with frothy bits of

white on top, like a soccer field that has a sprinkling of snow on it.

Kuantan may be a real one-horse town—that's what Dad calls it; I have no idea why, since I haven't ever seen even *one* horse—but living on the coast is fantastic.

The sun is warm on our backs. Rajiv and I run down to the water. My dad starts yelling immediately. He's so worried about us drowning that we're not allowed to go any farther than waist deep.

Mom is unpacking the picnic under the shade of a casuarina tree. When it's ready, she waves her arms frantically, like a coach trying to attract the referee's attention because he needs to bring on an extra striker to save the game.

We trudge up through the sand, sit cross-legged on the mat, and stuff our faces.

Another odd thing about Mom and Dad: For all the years we've lived in Kuantan, we've had a picnic by the sea every Saturday unless Dad is away on business or something.

How come we do family things together and have a great time and yet every evening Mom and Dad start yelling at each other again?

I run back down to the water, lie on the sand, and watch the waves swirling around my feet.

Amamma walks slowly down to the sea.

I really hope she's not planning to swim.

Fat chance.

It's quite a sight. She walks into the water with her arms held up straight even though the water is not past her ankles yet. Maybe she's worried about a big wave.

She has no bathing suit. Mom says Indian women as old as Amamma would never wear anything that showed too much arm or leg or tummy, so she's wearing her white sari.

Amamma keeps walking, her sari billowing like a collection of large mushrooms. The drape over her shoulder fans out on the surface of the water. After a while, the six yards of cloth (that's about how long a sari is) gets waterlogged and begins to sink.

Amamma walks slowly back to the shore and beckons to my father. "I'm wet now. Time to go."

We pack and leave. This is why it's annoying when Amamma decides to get in the water. She stays in for only five minutes because her sari gets wet and sandy and she is uncomfortable, but then we have to go home, since she won't change clothes on the beach.

And she's really nasty to sit next to in the car as she creates puddles on the back seat. If you complain, she says you have no respect for the elderly because you've been badly brought up by your mother.

At home we stand outside while Dad turns the garden hose on us. He doesn't like sand inside—it scratches the wooden floors. Dad watches Amamma walk into the house, and I wish he'd turn the hose on her too. Wouldn't that be funny?

He looks at me, and I can see he's guessed my thoughts. He smiles and shakes his head. He's probably right. She might have a heart attack. It wouldn't be right for him to kill his mother-in-law. Is it murder if you kill people by turning a garden hose on them?

CHAPTER
ELEVEN

I get my soccerball that evening. Mom says it is part of my next birthday present. That's fine with me. I won't even *need* a birthday present now that I've got my ball.

It's the most beautiful thing I've ever seen. It's round and made up of black and white pentagons and hexagons. How did the person who invented the soccerball know that a whole lot of pentagons and hexagons could be stitched together into a ball shape?

It's firm to the touch yet soft, like a watermelon wrapped in cotton. It smells of new shoes.

I hug it to my chest.

What more could a girl want?

A shirt and shorts? Cleats, perhaps, and shin guards. Well, maybe not shin guards. I want to be like Zico and wear my socks around my ankles.

It's time to practice.

. . .

Learning soccer skills is much harder than I thought it would be. The ball is heavy and hurts my toes, even inside my sneakers. I try running with it: I step on it, my foot rolls over the top, and I come crashing down.

This is *so* humiliating. I'm glad Rajiv is inside, watching TV.

I get up and try running with the ball again. This time it escapes and rolls ahead, and I am not so much dribbling as chasing it until it comes to a stop against the back fence.

Mom leans out the kitchen window and shouts, "Are you doing it right?"

I ignore her. This is what practice is about.

Even Zico must have started somewhere.

I settle for knocking the ball against a wall over and over again. Well, perhaps not over and over again. My record for the evening is three bounces.

Even Zico must have started *somewhere.*

That evening, France loses to Germany in the semifinal —on penalties. The Germans are going to win the World Cup once more. Don't they ever get tired of playing boring, defensive soccer?

In the darkness, I can hear Mom and Dad. They are yelling about Amamma ruining our picnic that morning. I know she was annoying, but surely not enough for two grownups to fight over?

CHAPTER
TWELVE

I wake up the next morning with the dawn prayers.

The mosque is not far from here—on the other side of a row of houses and a monsoon drain. The call to prayer is played through loudspeakers attached to the shiny gold-topped minaret five times a day, the first one at dawn and the last at dusk. We've all learned to sleep through it in the morning, even Dad.

I guess I was so excited about my new soccerball that I slept lightly for a change. My head is full of dreams of glory.

I grab the ball and run downstairs, listening to the prayers. They are almost like songs, except without music and in Arabic.

I said that once to Dad.

He said, "We'll never be able to sell the house."

Why would we want to sell the house anyway? It's our home. There's the monsoon drain—wider than a stream and deeper than a grave—to fish in and a yard for practicing soccer.

And Mom can grow fruit trees—a cow got in last week and ate all the saplings—and roses, which is almost impossible to do in Kuantan's sandy soil, but it has become personal for her.

Dad doesn't do any gardening, though he can spend hours sweeping up the sickle-shaped leaves that fall into the yard from the acacia trees along the monsoon drain.

We live near the sea. There is always a strong wind blowing. There hasn't been a single day in our lives when the yard didn't have as many leaves the next morning as Dad swept up the previous day.

"Why do you do it, Dad?" I asked him once.

He was shirtless, pouring with sweat, and chewing on a twig.

He took the twig out of his mouth, had a fit of coughing, gulped a glass of coconut water, and wheezed. "Keeps me healthy!"

Yeah, right.

I practice kicking the ball against the wall. Up to four bounces. I decide that when I get to ten, I'll try dribbling again.

My plan to train all day is ruined by Mom coming downstairs and reminding me that we're going to Kuala Lumpur, the capital of Malaysia, for the wedding of one of my cousins.

"Do I have to come, Mom?"

"Yes."

"Can I bring the ball?"

Mom sighs.

I know what's bugging her. Our large and nosy family will see soccer as the latest weirdness of her daughter.

"Please, Mom?"

"All right," says Mom.

The drive to Kuala Lumpur is long. It takes about five hours. At least Dad can see over the steering wheel. We spend a lot of time following the smoggy trail of timber trucks, with logs piled high on the back.

The logs are held in place by metal chains.

Every time we pass a timber truck, Mom says, "I hope those chains don't snap." I hope that too, as we'd be crushed by the logs rolling off it.

Passing is dangerous, not just because of the risk of falling logs. There's always someone coming the other way and trying to pass his own smog-spewing monster truck, so there's a lot of swerving back at the last minute to avoid head-on collisions.

Every thirty kilometers or so, we see an abandoned wreck by the side of the road. Dad says the driver didn't manage to swerve back in time. The police leave the wrecks as a warning to others to drive carefully, but it doesn't seem to be working.

The road bends so much that until I was eight years old, Mom used to carry plastic bags for me in case I threw up. I don't get carsick anymore, but we still sing during the winding parts to distract us. Usually "The Bear Went Over the Mountain" and "She'll Be Coming Round the Mountain."

There's a lot of puffing uphill and then speeding down the

other side. Kuantan and Kuala Lumpur are on opposite sides of a great mountain range that runs down the country like a poky spine.

We stop at Karak, a town so small, it makes Kuantan look like a bustling city. We always stop at Karak because Dad's favorite Indian restaurant is there, in a grubby row of shops along the road. Even though he's white, Dad loves Indian food. He knows where the best Indian restaurant is on every main street of every small town in Malaysia.

He used to say that he married Mom so she could cook Indian food for him every day.

That was when they still made jokes about their marriage.

We stuff our faces, eating from the banana leaves that South Indian restaurants use instead of plates.

After that, we sit in the car in silence. I'm too full to talk. Rajiv is asleep. Mom and Dad are getting tense because these family weddings can be difficult.

CHAPTER
THIRTEEN

Maya, you're growing so tall!" exclaims one of my aunts. "Isn't she growing so tall?" she asks a motley crew of relatives.

There are quick shakes of the head and sideways glances.

I grit my teeth and hold fast to my soccerball.

That was *not* a compliment. For a girl, being tall is like being dark. It's bad because no one will marry you—and that's all these people think about. Even when you're only eleven.

"Are you carrying the ball for your brother? What a helpful girl!"

I bounce the ball and say defiantly, "It's mine."

"Oh! Yours? . . . I thought it was a soccerball."

"It is."

"Oh . . ."

My brother walks in.

"Rajiv, you're growing so tall!"

The nods and murmurs are approving. Boys are encouraged to be tall and play soccer.

Mom sits inside with the women. She's wearing a silk sari with lots of gold thread.

Dad stands outside, talking to the men. That's what the men do at Indian weddings. They aren't even expected to dress up.

I'm forced to change into a pink dress with ruffles around the neck.

Rajiv looks at me and laughs. "You look like a flamingo!"

I don't bother to get angry. He's right. I look like a pink bird that stands on one leg.

When I get a chance, I practice with my ball in the yard. The pink dress turns all sweaty. The relatives watch me from the windows. I can see their lips moving as they mutter to each other.

My brother shouts from the porch where he is playing cards with some of the cousins, "Flamingoes don't play soccer!"

This one does.

CHAPTER
FOURTEEN

The wedding takes forever. We're at the temple in an area next to the main courtyard. The courtyard has lots of statues of different gods. There's Ganesha, with the head of an elephant; Shakti, with lots of arms; and Shiva, smiling mysteriously like the Mona Lisa.

The music is immensely loud. There are sitars (Indian guitars), dholaks (two-sided drums), and trumpets. I am tempted to stick my fingers in my ears. It sounds like the traveling bands at soccer matches: loud, tuneless, and enthusiastic.

The bride and groom are sitting on a raised red and gold pedestal. The priest is wearing a white sarong (a long piece of fabric wrapped around his waist) and not much else. He has smears of white dust on his chest and arms. Dad says it's burned cow dung. I really, seriously hope he's joking. The priest has long hair tied in a topknot and is muttering Sanskrit prayers over a small flame. Hardly anyone has any idea what he's saying. The women are gossiping among themselves, and the men are outside.

Even the couple getting married have no idea what's going on. Every time they're supposed to do something, one of the older uncles translates the Sanskrit into Tamil and then another uncle translates the Tamil into English—the groom doesn't even speak Tamil. I can't help wondering what will happen when all these old uncles who have some notion of what's happening aren't around anymore.

If weddings are no longer possible, maybe my relatives will be less worried about whom I'm going to marry.

At last the music reaches a crescendo, everyone stands up, the groom ties a gold chain around his bride's neck, uncooked rice is chucked at them (that bit is fun except it stings if you're in the firing line of some old relative with rolls of fat on her throwing arm), and it's all over.

The journey home isn't great. Mom and Dad are ticked off at each other.

Dad is complaining. "I can't stand these family things."

"It was a wedding—we had to go."

"All they do is talk about what car to buy and the housing market."

"Maybe if *we* had some money like the rest of them, it wouldn't annoy you so much!"

"And I wish they'd stop picking on Maya," continues Dad, replacing the toothpick in his mouth with a fresh one and chucking the old one out the window.

Mom doesn't say anything. I hug my soccerball to my chest. I wish they'd stop picking on me too.

D ad quit aid work a few years back. He says he wasn't helping anyone, it was all politics, and he couldn't stand it anymore. And besides, with two children, he needed to think about earning some money.

Since then he's started a whole lot of different businesses. He tried opening an Indian restaurant. It was doomed from the beginning—even I knew that. Who would go to an Indian restaurant owned by an Englishman? They'd be afraid of getting curried fish and chips. (Mom says you really do get curried fries at Indian restaurants in England, but I can hardly believe it.)

Next he opened a hobby shop, the kind that sells those unbelievably expensive toys, like miniature railway sets and mechanized racing cars.

Nobody in Kuantan has any money or time for hobbies.

Rajiv and I still play in the garage with all the leftover stock.

We can both construct a great Airfix World War II Spitfire—we've had so many model kits to practice with.

Right now, Dad's running a flying club. He has two small Cessna planes. They have names (actually radio call signs), *Victor Romeo* and *Uniform Romeo*. He's got a pilot's license, and he does crop dusting and joy rides. Sometime he lets my brother or me hold the controls and pilot the plane. Mom would freak out if she knew, so we don't tell her.

It's pretty special being part of the sky with your dad, even if he's hopeless at business.

That side of Dad doesn't bother me too much. But it's one of the things Mom and Dad fight about. She says he's irresponsible to keep risking the house on his stupid business ideas. She can't stand not knowing if we'll have money for school fees and food and stuff. She says it's embarrassing because the bank manager is one of our relatives and everyone knows we're broke.

Not having enough money does get a bit hairy sometimes.

Once, we were on the way to school and got stuck at a traffic light.

A huge man with a massive belly hanging over his trousers pulled up next to us on his scooter and yanked open Mom's car door.

I thought he was a robber and started screaming. It turned out he was there to take the Volvo back because Dad hadn't been paying for it every month the way he was supposed to.

Mom gave the man a bunch of money from her purse and he went away.

I was surprised.

I thought Dad must surely owe the car dealer more than that if they were worried enough to try to take the car away at a traffic light in the middle of rush hour. Mom didn't want to talk about it. Not to us anyway. Rajiv told me afterward that Mom wasn't paying for the car; she was just paying the man to go away.

The yelling upstairs that night felt louder than a stadium full of excited Brazilians.

CHAPTER
SIXTEEN

I'm going to England for a couple of weeks," says Dad.

We all react differently.

Mom says, "I hope you're not chasing some other daft business idea."

Rajiv shouts, "But I have a hockey game next week—you're supposed to come!"

I say, "Can you get me some books?" Dad always gets me books when he goes to England.

Dad scowls at Mom. He ruffles Rajiv's hair and says, "I'll be there next time, son."

Then he looks at me. "Are you still reading? I thought it was all soccer practice nowadays."

I say impatiently, "Don't be silly, Dad."

"At least she doesn't always have her nose in a book anymore." This was Mom's contribution.

Dad says, "Make me a list and I'll see what I can do."

Kuantan doesn't have a bookstore. There is a shop that stocks a few kids' books. But the owner, Mr. Hamid, buys new titles only when he has sold every single book. About a year ago, he opened his crate and discovered he'd ordered ten copies of *Five Run Away Together* by mistake. Three have been sold so far. I'm going to have to wait a long time before he brings in any new stuff.

But when Dad goes to England, Christmas comes early.

I make him a long list by copying out every single title from the back pages of my other books. It doesn't matter if I've never heard of the book or it has a weird name like *The Phantom Tollbooth* or *The Faraway Tree*.

Dad told me that when he gets to London, he goes straight to a bookstore called Foyles on Charing Cross Road, where books are piled high on every surface, and hands over the list.

At Foyles, they always have *everything*.

It must be the most amazing place in the whole world. Someday, I will go there. Dad's promised.

It can take a while for Dad to deliver on a promise, but I'm sure i'll get to visit Foyles eventually.

Rajiv is still sulking. "You *said* you'd come to the game, Dad."

"I know, Rajiv. But this is the only time I can go."

I know what that means. Dad's made a bit of money and needs to use it before someone takes it from him.

Mom says, "I'll come for the game."

"It's not the same," says Rajiv, and storms out of the room.

Dad sighs. Mom sighs.

I know where this is going.

I grab my soccerball. I need to put in some extra hours of practice so I'll have time to read when the books arrive.

CHAPTER
SEVENTEEN

The next morning, I take my ball to school. I decide against carrying it under my arm—that would attract too much attention.

I find a large paper bag and squeeze the ball in. The bag tears slightly along the seams.

At recess, I go down to the playground, rip the bag, drop the ball on the ground, and put one foot on it. I hope it looks like I know what I'm doing.

I fold my arms to appear determined.

"Anyone fancy a kick around?" I ask, my heart thumping against my chest so hard, it feels like it's trying to escape.

"We don't play soccer at this school," points out Susan, who is very good at netball. "Soccer is a *boys'* game."

"There's nothing to stop us from having a game at recess," I say urgently, looking at the other girls.

Nurhayati, who is very rich and very beautiful, says, "I'm not playing a boys' game." She tosses her head and walks away.

Most of the others hurry after her. I'm not surprised. A lot of the girls follow Nurhayati's lead. She is the most popular kid in our year. And her dad is the mayor of our small town. She comes to school in a big black limo driven by a chauffeur who opens the car door for her.

I swallow a sigh before it escapes. I feel like a coach whose two star players are home with the flu.

It was always a long shot, persuading any of the girls to play with me. But I had hoped *someone* would join me in a kick around.

I sit down on the ball with my arms around my knees.

A shadow falls over me, and I turn to squint at the person getting in my light.

It's Sok Mun. She says, "I'd like to play soccer."

Inside, I'm jumping up and down, but I act casual so she doesn't get spooked. I can hardly believe my luck. I have someone to pass the ball to now!

CHAPTER
EIGHTEEN

Our first practice is not very successful.

Sok Mun has no idea what to do.

I kick the ball toward her.

When it reaches her, she screams and backs away. I explain that she has to trap it or knock it back to me. She puts a foot on the ball and falls down.

On our next attempt, she hurts her toe. I explain that the ball is hard, so she really needs to use the side of her foot to kick it. "Otherwise, you're going to lose a toenail, Sok Mun."

Sok Mun makes a face to show how gross she thinks the idea is. But you've got to give the girl credit. She sticks with it right through recess.

Batumalar is watching us from under a frangipani tree. She's had another bad morning. She was late and her school shirt was wrinkled.

Sister Pauline is sure God prefers clothes that are well

ironed, so Batumalar got squats, lines, and a smack on the hand with a ruler.

I wave to Batumalar, inviting her to join us. I don't really want her to come over. She's a big girl and looks clumsy. I doubt that she's ever even seen a match. Mom says they don't have televisions in the workers' quarters of the plantations. Also, I'm afraid that if I spend time with her, I might get picked on too. I know us minorities should stick together, but I'm scared. I don't want anyone to pick on me.

Batumalar looks embarrassed to be caught watching and hurries away. I feel bad now for not wanting her to join Sok Mun and me. She doesn't have any friends at all. She's always alone at recess. Why am I such a coward? I feel like a penalty taker who at the last minute refuses to take the spot kick.

I am not concentrating on the ball. Sok Mun finally manages a side-footed, straight-to-me pass and the ball rolls between my legs.

Just my luck—Nurhayati is walking by at that moment. "You should turn professional, Maya," she sneers.

I pretend not to hear her, but I bet she can see that my ears and the back of my neck are as red as a setting sun.

CHAPTER
NINETEEN

Argentina versus West Germany.

South American flair versus plodding Europeans; that's what the newspapers are calling it.

It is not a difficult World Cup final in which to choose sides.

I am desperately worried, though. On paper, Argentina is far and away the better team, and they have the best player of this World Cup — Maradona.

But the Germans *always* win.

"They didn't win World War I or World War II," points out Rajiv.

"They haven't lost anything since then."

"I might watch the game," remarks Rajiv.

I throw him a grateful look.

Dad is in England. Mom only ever wakes up if she can cheer for the team playing *against* England.

And nobody should have to watch the World Cup final alone.

Rajiv continues, "The Germans are going to need some support."

I stare at him. I can't believe what I'm hearing.

"You wouldn't," I say.

He would.

He is actually going to cheer for Germany. I can't believe he's my brother. There must have been a mix-up at the hospital. I remember that Rajiv has Granddad's nose. All right, the mix-up must have been over me. I wonder where my real family is and whether they're all sitting together in their replica sky-blue and white striped shirts supporting Argentina.

I am lost in a daydream where my real parents don't quarrel and my real brother doesn't always support the other team.

The whistle to kick off the game drags me back to the present. The Germans are marking Maradona well. He is struggling to get in the game, but a defender, José Luis Brown, scores: 1–0!

I dance around the room. Rajiv steals my blanket. I don't care. Maybe it will turn out all right in the end.

Ten minutes into the second half, Valdano scores for Argentina: 2–0.

I can relax now. My brother is slumped on the sofa, looking

bored. He really isn't interested in soccer, so if he's not needling me, he's not having fun.

He knows that not even the Germans are going to come back from *two* goals down.

The Germans come back from two goals down.

Rummenigge and Völler both score: 2–2.

I can't believe it. There are only ten minutes left. There's no way that Argentina would win a penalty shootout. Not against the Germans. Ask the English. Ask the French. Ask every single team that has been knocked out of tournaments by the Germans on penalties.

Rajiv is dancing around the room. I steal the blanket back.

But the Germans have gotten ahead of themselves. They know they're unbeatable on penalties. They're dreaming of a famous victory.

They forget to watch Maradona.

He picks up the ball and slides it through to Jorge Burruchaga. Burruchaga scores: 3–2!

The whistle blows.

Even Rajiv is jumping up and down. What a final! What a World Cup!

I hate it that Brazil was eliminated in the quarterfinals and my Zico will never win a World Cup medal—but there's no denying that Maradona and Argentina deserve their win.

Maradona is kissing the golden trophy. Tears are streaming down his cheeks.

I feel my eyes go all prickly. I rub them hard with my knuckles. There'll be time enough for tears of happiness when I turn professional and win my own World Cup.

CHAPTER
TWENTY

The practicing is going well.

I have mastered a step over. I put my right foot against the ball so it looks like I am going to kick it. Then I step over the ball with my left foot, as if I'm going the other way. At the last moment, I flick the ball around the left of the defender with my right foot and sprint past on his right side.

At least, I think that's what I do.

I don't have any defenders to play against, but I get Mom to stand in the middle of the yard and let me go around her. She doesn't try to take the ball off me, so I can do the whole trick in slow motion. I assume that I will speed up with practice.

The ball rolls into the monsoon drain. By the time I have climbed in and recovered it, Mom is weeding the flower beds. She has substituted herself with a potted rosebush.

I bet that never happened to Zico.

The thorny rosebush is a better defender than Mom. If I get

confused with my step over and run straight into it, it really hurts!

I bet that never happened to Zico either.

At school, I'm making progress. Sok Mun has learned to pass to me and also not to scream when she receives the ball. A few other girls hang around and watch us play. One or two of them kick the ball back if it rolls to where they're lurking.

I come up with a cunning plan. I pretend to miskick the ball, but I actually knock it in their direction quite often. In a while, almost without realizing it, they're playing too.

We are five now. Half a team, excluding the goalie!

Batumalar doesn't watch us anymore. I don't know where she is. I need to do something about her, but I have no idea what. What would Zico do in this situation?

I decide to look for her after practice and persuade her to join the team. It is the right thing to do, and kids in books always manage to do that, so I'll try too. She might play well in goal. She looks strong with her square face and square shoulders.

But Batumalar is nowhere to be found. I look for her in the lunchroom, by the frangipani trees, and in the small playground with the climbing frame. It is supposed to be for the small kids, but the big girls always sit on top and gossip and scowl at anyone under twelve.

There is no sign of her.

In the end I give up. The bell will ring any second now for the end of recess. I know I will not approach Batumalar in class, about soccer or anything else. I don't have the guts to be her friend.

That evening, Rajiv is still complaining about Dad missing his hockey game.

"He's never missed one before," he grumbles.

"But he's busy in England, Rajiv," I remind him. "It's not that big a deal."

"The other dads will be there. I'll be the only kid without one. It's the season final. I just can't believe it."

Rajiv is quite a good hockey player. His team is playing in the interschool, under-sixteen Kuantan division final. If they win, Rajiv will get to take part in a big tournament in Kuala Lumpur with all the other schools that topped their divisions.

I still think hockey is a stupid game.

But at least Rajiv is doing the thing properly.

I realize that the next step in my soccer career is to find a team to play against.

We won't be ready for a while, but it is important to plan ahead.

CHAPTER
TWENTY-ONE

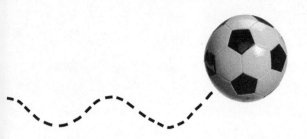

Dad is back.

I am thrilled to see him. He can barely carry his suitcase into the house. I hope it's weighed down with books.

Rajiv is trying to look offended, but he can't manage it. He's so pleased that Dad is home. The tip of his nose is bright red, which is what happens when he is happy. He looks like a soccer player who's just been told that his knee injury, which he thought would rule him out for the rest of the season, is a minor matter and he'll be up and running in a few days.

Mom is still in the house. She never comes out when Dad gets back from a trip. It sounds strange, but I guess she's just not that excited to see him. It's silly of me to expect anything else. Whenever Rajiv and I are mad at each other, like now because he supported Germany in the World Cup final, neither of us can stop trying to annoy the other. Sometimes Rajiv even sticks a foot out to trip me.

How much worse must it be for Mom and Dad, who have been mad at each other for most of the years I've been alive.

I guess I should be grateful that they're not sticking a leg out trying to trip each other.

Rajiv sticks a leg out now, but I'm in training to be a professional soccer player. I skip over his leg as if he's a despairing last defender.

Dad says, "Rajiv," in a warning voice.

I decide not to let Rajiv spoil Dad's first evening home.

"It's all right, Dad. He missed! Which books did you get for me?"

Dad is distracted and unzips his suitcase.

Rajiv grins at me — truce.

Mom finally comes out of the kitchen.

They don't speak directly to each other, Mom and Dad.

"Look, Mom. Look at the books Dad got me!"

I drag them out of the Foyles bags in a rush, shouting out titles. "It's *To Kill a Mockingbird* and all the *Secret Seven* books and" — I stop to glare at Dad — "*Five Run Away Together*. Dad, I have this one!"

"Sorry, honey. I must have got confused, or maybe Foyles did."

He ruffles my hair and I hug him around his expanding waist.

"That's all right, Dad. Thank you! You're the best dad in the whole world!"

I see Mom's face as I say that. She is smiling to see me so happy, but her funny, twisty smile gives me a pain in my chest.

My smile becomes twisty too. I can feel my lips turn down at the corners. My arms are still around Dad's waist and he is laughing with pleasure, but I have a really weird feeling that things are about to get plain awful.

Mom says, "Dinner is on the table."

Dad says, "I could really use a good Indian meal—it's been fish and chips out of old newspapers for days!"

Rajiv and I catch each other's eye and I see the hope in my eyes reflected in his.

Maybe things are going to be all right, and that sinking feeling, like an out-of-position defender watching a striker on a hat trick skip around the goalie, was just indigestion or something.

I say in a cheerful voice that almost catches in my throat, "I'm hungry too."

CHAPTER
TWENTY-TWO

Juggling a soccerball on a knee or a foot and then flicking it up and landing it on the back of your neck takes real skill. So does taking part in a conversation among four people without speaking directly to one of them. But Mom and Dad can do it.

Rajiv and I ask Dad questions about his trip and he answers us. Mom listens but doesn't say anything. If I ask her a question about what Dad is talking about, she answers. He doesn't talk over her or ignore her, and she doesn't do that to him either. If you didn't know better or weren't paying attention, it would seem like a normal dinnertime conversation.

I ask, "Dad, did you watch the World Cup final?"

"Yes, great game."

"I was supporting Argentina," I say smugly. "Rajiv was cheering for Germany."

"Were you now? Was it just to annoy your sister?"

Rajiv nods and grins.

"Who were you supporting, Dad?" I ask.

"It was tough—no Englishman can support Germany!"

"But what about the Falklands? Mom says that you were at war with Argentina too! Right, Mom?"

"Yes, dear."

"It's true, we were," says Dad, making a face as if he's just gotten a yellow card for a dangerous tackle.

"So which team were you cheering for?" I ask impatiently. I just want an answer to a simple question about whether Dad and I were on the same side. I don't need a history lesson about every war England has fought with another soccer-playing nation.

"Well," says Dad, putting on his thoughtful face, "I had to choose the old-fashioned way—picking the team that played the best soccer!"

"That was Maradona and Argentina!" I exclaim.

"It was indeed," he says, and we grin happily at each other.

CHAPTER
TWENTY-THREE

That night there is no yelling. I am up reading one of my new books, *Two Weeks with the Queen*. When I get out of bed for a pee I notice that Mom and Dad's bedroom light is still on.

They're up, but they're not yelling . . . that's strange.

I don't think about it too much because I'm anxious to get back to my book.

The next day is Saturday.

At breakfast, Mom and Dad look really tired—as if they haven't slept at all. Mom's hair is all over the place and Dad's eyes are red. Usually it's Mom's eyes that are red in the morning if they've been fighting. I hope things haven't gotten to the stage where Dad is crying too.

We eat in silence.

I don't like this sort of quiet—it's like a stadium full of

people observing a minute's silence because someone important has died. It's quiet, but it's sad and tense as well.

Usually I'd talk to fill the empty spaces, but today I just don't seem to be able to do it.

After breakfast Mom picks up our plates and puts them in the sink.

Dad clears his throat.

We look at him, but he doesn't say anything.

Mom sits back down, which is strange. She normally just washes the dishes.

"Kids, we have something to tell you," says Dad.

We turn to look at Dad, but he just looks at Mom.

She runs her hands through her hair and smiles a twisty smile.

She says, "You probably won't be happy when you hear the news, but in the long run I think you'll understand it's for the best."

What is she talking about? And why has she fallen silent before actually *telling* us the news?

Dad takes over. "You know your mom and I have been having a tough time."

"What do you mean, Dad?"

Rajiv pipes up. "Are we out of money again?"

I remember all the books Dad bought me at Foyles. They must have cost a small fortune.

"If the books were too expensive, I could ask Mr. Hamid at the shop if he wants to buy them." I hate offering to give up my books, but it seems like the right thing to do. I don't want to raise their hopes that Mr. Hamid will solve our money problems, so I add, "But he still has some copies of *Five Run Away Together,* so he might not be interested."

Dad does the twisty smile thing. Can you believe it? It must be catching.

He says, "No, it's not about money."

Mom says, "Sometimes grownups who are married to each other aren't that happy."

Does she think Rajiv and I are blind and deaf?

"We know that, Mom!"

"It is important for you to know that it doesn't mean we don't love the two of you. It's just your dad and I who have problems."

Dad adds, "It has nothing to do with you."

"Is it because you're white and Mom's Indian?" I demand.

"Of course not," he replies. "That's the least of our problems."

He half smiles at Mom as if he's remembering better days.

Rajiv is rocking his chair back and staring down at the table.

Usually, Dad gets cross when Rajiv rocks his chair. Today, he says nothing. This is not good.

I look from Mom to Dad and from Dad to Mom.

They both seem really sad.

"What's going on?" I ask. "What are you trying to say?"

"Your dad and I are getting a divorce."

CHAPTER
TWENTY-FOUR

I wait for Rajiv to say something, but he's just rocking his chair, back and forth, back and forth.

It's as if I've been given a red card even though it's the other guy who head-butted me in the chest, and I'm so winded, I can't speak to explain to the referee that it's all a terrible misunderstanding.

Mom says, "It isn't about you kids. Your dad and I have just decided that we can't be together anymore."

I finally find my tongue. "But what does that *mean?*"

Dad says, "I'm going back to England."

CHAPTER
TWENTY-FIVE

R ajiv's chair stops mid-rock. He's too far back, so the chair tumbles and he has to twist out of it. He lands on his hands and knees.

He gets slowly to his feet. The chair is lying on its back.

Mom, who leaped up as he fell over, asks, "Are you all right?"

That is such a dumb question.

Dad is just looking at Rajiv.

Rajiv asks, "What about us?"

Mom says, "You'll both stay with me here in Kuantan. You'll see your dad as often as possible, of course."

"But Amamma said this would never happen!"

Rajiv quoting Amamma is like a manager sending in a sub with two broken legs, an act of pure desperation.

"Divorce is unusual in our community," says Mom, almost in a whisper, as if she fears Amamma might hear her even though she's with one of my uncles at the moment. "But it does happen."

"And I know you children would want your mom and me to have a last chance at happiness rather than staying together just to save your grandmother a bit of embarrassment."

Last chance at happiness? Did Dad really just say that?

"But why do you have to go to England?" I ask. I know I'm speaking because I can hear the words and they're in my "squeaky with worry" voice. I am so numb with shock, I would not be able to tell otherwise.

Dad mumbles, "I've found a job there. It's quite a good opportunity. You know the flying club is losing money —"

"But I'm sure you could find a job here," argues Rajiv. He is getting angry; his nose looks like a white flag, but he hasn't given up yet.

Dad stares at his feet and then he glances at both of us. He says, "I need to get away." His voice cracks a little. "Maybe I'll find a job back here when I've had a change of scene for a while."

My dad needs a *change of scene*—from his family. From Mom and Rajiv and me. My dad, who takes us to the beach every weekend, who lets us fly his little plane, who bought me a ton of books at Foyles, needs a change of scene for his *last chance at happiness*.

I can't believe what I'm hearing.

I feel as if I've just scored an own goal in a tied match in the last minute of overtime.

CHAPTER
TWENTY-SIX

Dad leaves in a month.

His last words as he gets into a taxi to take him to the airport are "I'll save some money and fly you guys out for Christmas. That will be great. Maybe we'll have snow!"

I have my soccerball under my arm and there are tears in my eyes. I prefer not to cry. I don't think it looks right for the "I'm too tough to wear shin guards" type of soccer player to cry except from happiness when winning a World Cup. But this is a special occasion. Probably even Zico would have cried.

Besides, if we have to wait for Dad to save enough money to fly us out to England, we'll probably never see him again.

CHAPTER
TWENTY-SEVEN

In some ways, it is easier at home without Dad. There is no arguing at night. There is no one at breakfast who does not speak to someone else, at least when Amamma isn't around.

And she's not around that much anymore.

She says it is *too* humiliating to have a daughter who couldn't even hang on to her own husband, not even a *white* husband. She'd rather spend time with my uncles. Lucky them.

But when I look at the yard and it is thick with leaves because Dad is not sweeping furiously, or we go to the beach on Saturdays and there is no one to yell at us if we get too deep, I have to bite my bottom lip hard because there is a huge hole in our lives where Dad used to be and nothing to fill it with.

Mom has gone back to work part-time. She says she just

feels more comfortable not having to wait for Dad's checks to arrive—they might get lost in the mail or something.

Who is she trying to kid, I wonder. We all know that if Dad's check doesn't arrive, it will have nothing to do with the postal system. Mom seems to have made up her mind that she won't say anything nasty about Dad now that he's gone.

I guess she thinks it will make it easier for us kids.

I wish she had thought of it earlier. Perhaps he wouldn't have left if she hadn't said nasty things to him before.

I know that's not fair. It's not really Mom's fault.

Rajiv is angry, though. He won't let Mom come to any of his hockey matches. I don't suppose he thinks it's Mom's fault either. I am sure he knows it takes two to argue. Mom smiles her twisty smile and pretends she doesn't mind. I guess none of us is fooling anyone about how we feel.

Nobody at school knows. I'm far too ashamed to admit that my dad has left us.

There's Sok Mun's dad working all hours at the fruit stall to make enough to feed the family, and Batumalar's dad bringing her in on a motor scooter every day so that she can attend a good school, and Nurhayati's dad about to run for reelection as mayor. They're sure to think there must be something about me or Rajiv or Mom that made Dad leave.

Maybe there *is* something wrong with us—I don't know. I mean, we must be pretty bad if Dad's last chance of happiness is on the other side of the world.

But I'm not telling anyone that Dad lives in England for now. And I know Rajiv isn't either. Our lips are sealed.

Unfortunately, people are bound to find out.

Kuantan is such a small town. I try not to think about the whispers and the stares when the news finally gets out. I can just imagine the girls pointing and nodding. "There's that kid whose father went to live in England. He needed a change of scene. I always thought there was something odd about that family . . ."

It's definitely time to practice with the soccerball.

My skills are improving. I can dribble around the rosebush and do a keepie-uppie thing with the ball on my knee and my foot—thirty-eight bounces is my new personal record.

The team is getting better as well. The five of us play every day, and we hardly ever miss a pass. Sok Mun has overcome her fear of the ball so well that she now plays in goal.

One morning, Mom drops me off just as Batumalar's dad arrives on his scooter with Batumalar on the back, her helmet strapped under her chin. He waits while she gets off.

I am walking past and I smile at them. I don't want her dad to realize that his daughter doesn't have any friends.

He speaks to me and I stare at him blankly. He is speaking in Tamil, and although it is my mother tongue, unless I'm saying no to a second helping of rice or Mom is asking if I want more dosa, my Tamil is embarrassing. At least Amamma says so, and she should know.

Batumalar's dad points to the ball under my arm and says in English, "You play soccer?"

I nod. If the other girls catch me being chatty to him, I'm finished.

Then I remember that at least Batumalar has a dad who doesn't need a change of scene, so I smile and say, "Yes, I love soccer."

"You must play with Batumalar," he says. "So she can be your good friend, yes?" He waves his arms around to emphasize the point. Does he think soccer is played with hands?

Batumalar tucks her fists into her pockets, but not before I notice that her hands are as big as soup plates.

"I will," I say. "I promise."

He disappears in a cloud of dust. I turn around, determined to ask Batumalar to join the team. She has gone ahead.

For once, she's on time.

I reach the classroom late and have to write lines.

CHAPTER
TWENTY-EIGHT

I speak to Dad on the phone once a week.

It doesn't really work that well.

He's always asking me what we're doing and how Rajiv and I are getting along.

But there's just not that much to tell.

I practice my soccer, read my books, argue with Rajiv, and worry about Batumalar being bullied (and me being too chicken to do anything about it).

It's just normal life. And normal life is not very interesting to talk about over the phone. Normal life is about *living* it with your dad.

It's not about telling him that you can flick the ball over your head with your heel and volley it into the goal. It's about running into the house the first time you do it and dragging him outside to see you try to repeat the trick.

It's not about telling him about the book you're reading. It's about Dad telling you to get your nose out of the book and do your homework.

It's not about describing a picnic that Amamma has ruined. It's about catching his eye when she's knee-deep in water and sharing a secret with an in-your-heart, not-out-loud giggle.

Rajiv refuses to speak to Dad on the phone.

After a while, Dad stops calling so often. There's no further mention of a visit at Christmas. Amamma, who is back with us for a visit, has perfected an "I told you so" roll of the eyes.

Mom says he's probably busy working hard at his new job. It's not that easy, settling down in a new place. Dad must have a lot on his mind.

That may be true, but it doesn't seem to include Rajiv and me.

CHAPTER
TWENTY-NINE

I t's a miracle!

Nurhayati wants to join the team.

"But why? I thought you said soccer was a boys' game."

Nurhayati tosses her head, and her long, beautiful hair flounces like she's in a shampoo ad.

"I've changed my mind, that's all."

I am still staring at her in amazement—as if she were a streaker who's run onto the soccer field naked.

"Well, can I play or not?"

I shake off my surprise and hold out my hand. She shakes it gingerly. "You're in!" I shout. Then I juggle the ball on my knee just to show her how much work she has to do to be as good as I am.

Later, Sok Mun tells me that Nurhayati really likes a boy who lives down the road from her, but he cares only about soccer. So she's decided to target his weak spot—and if that means she has to join our team, so be it.

Nurhayati being on the team makes *all* the difference.

Now the other kids want to play too, so we have no problem fielding an eleven-a-side team. In fact, we have so many volunteers, the team has subs on the bench!

Soccer might not be cool when *I* play it, but when Nurhayati is kicking the ball gingerly—as if it's a porcupine and not a ball —the girls are prepared to believe it might be fun.

I don't mind. At least we have a team. And I'm still the best player.

CHAPTER
THIRTY

It's time to think about uniforms—and matches against other teams.

I consider asking Sister Pauline, but she might think that God doesn't like girls playing soccer. I go to see the headmaster, Mr. de Cruz, instead.

"Yes, child?"

"The girls have formed a soccer team, sir, and I was wondering whether the school would get us some uniforms."

"Do you think money grows on trees, young lady?"

Actually I do, since money is made from paper and paper comes from trees, but my training with Amamma kicks in and I realize he's not looking for an honest answer.

"No, sir."

"That's right. We're on a tight budget here. Unless you think we should stop paying teachers and buy you uniforms instead?"

I would love it, love it, *love* it if he stopped paying Sister Pauline.

Instead, I say, "No, sir," and hurry out of his office before he does something truly awful, like ban soccer.

The others are waiting for me. I shake my head.

No money, no uniforms.

No uniforms, no matches.

No matches, no opportunity to score a winning goal with a bicycle kick at the far post and be spotted by a talent scout from a big team.

"We need to raise money," I tell the team.

"How?" asks Sok Mun. She looks worried.

"Not from our parents," I say hastily. "Does anyone have any ideas?"

They all shake their heads.

"How about a lemonade stand?" I ask.

"What's lemonade?" demands Nurhayati.

Fair point. I don't know either. It was just something I'd read about in a book. "I think it's like lime juice," I reply.

"Who'd pay for something we can make at home?"

I scowl at Nurhayati. She's like a referee whistling for every tiny foul and interfering with the flow of the game.

"How about we wash cars for money?"

"I don't have a car," points out Sok Mun.

"Other people's cars."

"My chauffeur washes our cars," says Nurhayati.

I remember that Rajiv and I wash our Volvo every Sunday and Mom has never paid us a penny for our work.

"Let's all go home and think of an idea and we'll discuss it again tomorrow," I said.

I tell Mom my troubles. She doesn't have a solution except to say she won't pay me to wash the car.

"I have a new hockey uniform from school," says Rajiv, "because we have a big tournament coming up."

"Well, the headmaster said we couldn't have any money."

"Because he doesn't want girls to play soccer," Amamma says. "Such a sensible man. Pity your mother didn't marry him instead of your no-good father."

I'm about to leap to Dad's defense when Rajiv grabs my arm.

"I have an idea," he says, grinning from ear to ear—the first time I've seen him smile that wide since Dad left.

CHAPTER
THIRTY-ONE

P lease tell us you're not serious."

The team is unanimous in their rejection of our new uniforms—hand-me-downs from Rajiv's hockey team that I have persuaded everyone to try on after school.

"Isn't it more important that we finally *have* a uniform than how it looks? Now we can compete! We can play matches!"

"Everything is much too big," complains Nurhayati.

I won't deny that we look ridiculous. Rajiv's teammates are between fourteen and sixteen years old. We are eleven. Rajiv's shorts reach my calves and look like a skirt. Rajiv's shirt covers my knees.

"Maybe if we tuck the shirts in," I say.

"There is no way I'll be seen dead—or alive—in this thing," says Nurhayati.

"That's what happens when you play soccer to impress boys instead of for the love of the beautiful game."

I really wish I had kept that thought to myself.

In a moment, we're all yelling at each other at the tops of our voices, and now my football team consists of eleven furious girls in baggy clothes.

None of us notices Nurhayati's father until he is standing right next to us.

"What's going on here?" he asks.

Suddenly, there is complete silence. He is the mayor, after all. The girls turn red or white except for Sok Mun, who is as gray faced as a cloudy sky.

"What in the world are you wearing, Nurhayati?"

She doesn't look at him.

"It's the new uniforms for our soccer team," I explain.

"From the school?"

"From my brother's hockey team."

"I see."

And I can tell he does because he tries very hard not to smile, which is kind of him under the circumstances.

"I think it would be better if you had uniforms in your, um, own size."

Does he think we are wearing this stuff by choice? My opinion of him goes down a couple of shirt sizes.

He puts an arm around Nurhayati's shoulder and I feel a lump in my throat. "Let me see what I can do," he says.

 urhayati is an only child, and her mega-rich dad gives her everything she wants.

And right now she wants to play soccer, although I suspect her father has no idea why.

First, he informs the headmaster that he expects all sports to get equal treatment—if the netball girls have uniforms, the soccer girls should have uniforms too—and that he himself will coach our team.

I persuade Nurhayati to ask for blue shorts, yellow jerseys, and white socks. The silly creature wants something in *pink,* but I explain to her carefully that pink won't impress the boy down the street, who is almost certainly a Brazil supporter.

"How do you know that?" she asks suspiciously.

"Everyone who knows anything about soccer supports Brazil," I explain.

She's not sure whether she believes me, but in soccer-related matters I have the upper hand.

We get the blue shorts, yellow jerseys, and white socks. We even get cleats and shin guards! We look fabulous, like a real team.

I wish Dad could see me in my new uniform. Mom loves it. Rajiv shrugs and pretends he doesn't think much of my outfit, but I bet he's secretly impressed—especially after I show him how silly I look in his old stuff.

Amamma says, "Already I cannot show my face in town because your father has run away and now this . . ."

CHAPTER
THIRTY-THREE

Nurhayati's dad wants us to play matches against other girls' teams.

But there aren't any.

The other girls' schools don't have soccer teams.

Nurhayati's dad, though, isn't a mayor running for reelection for nothing.

He arranges an interschool tournament through his office, and City Hall offers ten thousand ringgit (that's what you call the money in Malaysia) to the school that wins.

"It is my duty as mayor to encourage participation in sports," he says, "so that we have healthy and happy children in this town."

"That's what they do with our taxes," sniffs Amamma. "Waste it on nonsense like girls playing soccer. I'm not voting for that man ever again."

"You don't pay taxes," says Mom. "You get a pension from the government."

"So?"

"So some might call *that* a waste of taxpayer money."

I've noticed that Mom is much tougher with Amamma now that Dad has left.

Despite Amamma's opinions, the schools in Kuantan form girls' teams right away.

Ten thousand ringgit is a lot of money, and there are principals all over Kuantan dreaming of new desks and chairs and textbooks.

I am so excited. I feel like I've been picked as a member of Brazil's squad for a World Cup.

I hope Nurhayati's crush on this boy lasts long enough for us to take part in the tournament.

ad has stopped calling.

I find Rajiv smoking a cigarette by the monsoon drain when Mom is at work.

"What are you doing? Mom will kill you!"

"I'm old enough to do what I want."

"Rajiv, you're fourteen."

"I'm the man of the house now."

"Don't be silly. Just because Dad lives in England does not mean you're the head of anything."

Rajiv shrugs. He sucks in a lungful of smoke and coughs loudly.

Small fish in the drain scatter in alarm, but the tadpoles, fat blobs with small tails, stay where they are. The monsoon drain has only an inch of water at the bottom. But when the rains come, it will flow like a river. Without it we would be up to our knees in water in the living room for half the year.

I say, "Dad leaving didn't have anything to do with us."

"He doesn't even call anymore."

"He's just busy with the new job and all."

"Do you really believe that?"

I shrug. "And anyway, you won't speak to him when he does call."

I sit down next to him. I wish I dared to have a cigarette. When I think of Dad I am so angry that I would just love to do something that is totally, completely, absolutely against the rules. But cigarettes are bad for your health, and future professional soccer players have to be very careful about keeping fit.

So do hockey players.

"You need to keep healthy for hockey."

"I don't care about hockey."

I'm shocked. That's like me saying I don't care about soccer. Besides, I know that it isn't true. Rajiv is upset because he's the only kid who doesn't have a dad to come and watch his games.

I know how he feels.

My soccer tournament is next week, and Dad won't be there to see me. Can you believe it? My first competitive game ever and Dad won't be there.

Dad and I haven't spoken for so long that he doesn't even know about Nurhayati's dad organizing the event or getting us uniforms or anything.

I feel tears trickle down my cheeks.

"What's up?" Rajiv asks, looking away so that I won't be embarrassed.

"Dad won't be at my game either."

Rajiv takes the cigarette out of his mouth and chucks it in the drain. I watch the lit end fizzle out. The tadpoles come over to investigate.

"I'll come to the game," says Rajiv.

He puts an arm around my shoulders, and it reminds me of when Nurhayati's dad did the same to her. It's the first time Rajiv's ever done something like this.

He says again, "I'm the man of the house and I'll come for the game."

"I hope the tadpoles don't get poisoned by your cigarette," I say to hide how touched I am.

CHAPTER
THIRTY-FIVE

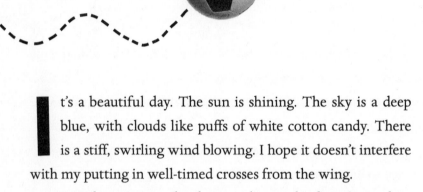

It's a beautiful day. The sun is shining. The sky is a deep blue, with clouds like puffs of white cotton candy. There is a stiff, swirling wind blowing. I hope it doesn't interfere with my putting in well-timed crosses from the wing.

Mom drives us to school. For a change she doesn't get close to hitting anything, so I can concentrate on being terrified.

Rajiv sits in the front with her. He's grinning with excitement. For this whole week, he's called me Zico.

Not Maya or Hey you or Idiot, but *Zico*.

He's a much better brother now that Dad is gone.

I'm dressed in my Brazil look-alike uniform. The numbers were stuck on yesterday. To my immense, heart-bursting pride, I've been given the number-10 jersey.

I don't know if scoring the winning goal in a World Cup final could feel better than having a number-10 jersey—the same number Zico wears, the same number Pelé used to wear. Even Maradona wears a 10.

To be honest, I'm not sure that the other girls know how important the number 10 is. But when Nurhayati's dad, who is now our unofficial coach, asked me if I wanted the number, I knew *he* understood what it meant.

I think it was really nice of him not to give it to his own daughter. It would have been silly, of course. She's an *awful* player. But on the other hand, without him there would be no team, no uniforms, no tournament, and no prize money. I'd have understood if he felt that Nurhayati should have the shirt.

"Hey, Zico, you excited?" asks Rajiv.

I nod. I don't dare speak because my heart is in my mouth and I don't want it to fall out.

I clutch my soccerball under my arm and we make our way to the hockey field. We're playing on a hockey field with hockey goals because Nurhayati's dad thinks the crowd might get bored waiting for an eleven-year-old to run the length of a soccer field. He might be right.

We're playing at our school, so we're the home team. I see lots of parents I don't recognize, though—away supporters, I suppose.

There are banners and flags and balloons.

There's a *phutphut* sound in the air and I look up.

It's *Uniform Romeo,* Dad's old plane, flying in circles overhead with thick clouds of colorful smoke trailing behind. It looks awesome. The new owners of the flying club must be putting on a show to attract customers.

Poor Dad. The minute he sells a business, someone else makes money from it.

I really miss him today.

The self-proclaimed "man of the house" is squinting at the plane too. He slaps me on the back.

"Time to warm up, Zico!"

Things begin to go wrong when we get to the field. The team is there, but no one looks happy.

Sok Mun is sitting on the ground holding her ankle with her goal-keeping gloves on.

"What's happened?" I ask.

Nurhayati says, "She's twisted her ankle."

Sok Mun takes one hand off her ankle to wipe away tears.

Her ankle is twice its normal size.

"I was just warming up and I fell down," Sok Mun says.

Nurhayati's dad arrives with an ice pack and some bandages. We watch him strap up her leg. He helps her to her feet. She stands on one leg, takes off the gloves, and says, "I'm sorry—I can't play."

Nurhayati's dad says, "No, you can't play. There'll be other tournaments, Sok Mun. You can watch the game with your mom and dad now."

Sok Mun says, "Good luck," and smiles at us. Then she hobbles toward the stands.

We watch her go in silence.

We don't have a goalie.

CHAPTER
THIRTY-SIX

We don't have a goalie.

We don't have a goalie!

We don't have a goalie!!

Fortunately, I am only screaming it in my head because otherwise we wouldn't have a goalie *or* a midfielder when I get dragged off to the funny farm.

Nurhayati's dad says, "We don't have a goalie."

I catch his eye. I suspect he feels like screaming too.

The thing is, we have a lot of substitutes, now that it's cool to play soccer in our school because Nurhayati does. But we don't have a spare goalie. That's because most of the girls, including me, just want a chance to score the winning goal in the final. Also, a lot of the girls don't like the idea of being in the line of fire when kids are taking pot shots at the goal from all over the field. Quite a few of my teammates have only recently stopped squealing when the ball rolls to them.

The other teams are warming up and laughing and waving to their parents in the crowd. We sit glumly in a circle.

Suddenly, I spot Batumalar. She is sitting in the stands with her dad.

I remember him flailing his arms and telling me that she should play too while she stuffed her big hands into her pockets.

I remember that I kept meaning to ask her to join the team.

I remember that I was too afraid to be her friend.

I remember that minorities have to stick up for each other.

I grab the goal-keeping gloves and leap to my feet.

"Where are you going?" asks Nurhayati.

"I think I've found us a goalie!"

I run up to the stands and wave the gloves in her face. "Batumalar, Sok Mun is injured! Will you be our goalie?"

Batumalar refuses point-blank. She doesn't say anything. She just looks at the ground while shaking her head furiously.

Everyone in the crowd is watching us and wondering what's going on.

Even under her dark skin, I see that Batumalar has gone brick red.

Her dad says something to her in Tamil. I have no idea what it is.

Then he says, "You have to try."

I understand this bit of Tamil because my aunts are always telling me I have to try some new dish they've cooked. They say, "How will you know whether you like it or not if you don't try?"

Batumalar is still shaking her head.

For the first time in my life, I try to speak Tamil to a stranger. I say, "You have to try."

She looks stunned.

I guess she didn't realize I could speak Tamil. Or maybe I said something like "You have to stand on one foot while squawking like a chicken." I don't know.

Either way, she grabs the gloves and stands up.

Her dad stands up too and gives her an awkward pat on the back. He's beaming with pride.

I feel so jealous of her and her dad that I almost grab the gloves back.

Batumalar and I are not a minority of two. I'm a minority of one, the only kid who doesn't have a dad at the tournament to cheer her on.

But then I hear Rajiv yelling, "Hurry up, Zico. What are you waiting for?"

I grab Batumalar by the hand and we race down to the field.

CHAPTER
THIRTY-SEVEN

There are two groups of four teams.

I watch them warm up. It looks like most of the girls have been playing only since the prize money was announced.

We win the first game 9–0 against a school from down the street. I score six of the nine goals, and Batumalar pulls off two fine saves.

She is an absolutely fabulous goalie. She springs from one side of the goal to the other as if she's . . . on springs! She can reach the top corners. She's a Peter Shilton — solid, dependable, and athletic. She has great composure too. She seems so calm and so large. The other team gives up almost before taking a shot. I don't blame them.

At their end, the goalie is a small eleven-year-old wishing she was somewhere else. When the ball comes toward her, she moves out of the way. It's mean of us to put nine goals past her. As Dad might say, "It's like shooting fish in a bucket."

I wish I hadn't thought about Dad.

CHAPTER
THIRTY-EIGHT

T he tournament is set up so that the top two teams in each group will go through to the semifinals.

We're winning all our games by five-goal margins. Our group is certain to finish in first place.

But on the other side of the draw, there is a team from Beserah Girls' School doing really well too.

It soon becomes clear that the final will be between them and us.

I watch them in their semifinal. I wonder whether the teachers have cheated and sneaked some boys onto the team. I stare hard. The players don't look like boys. They have ponytails, and some of them are very pretty. I suspect they have soccer-playing brothers or fathers.

They don't score as many goals as us but they defend well. It's like watching Germany. They're even wearing black shorts and white tops like the German national team.

I'm getting really nervous. They might beat us.

Nurhayati's dad announces the final. It will be between my school and Beserah, the two unbeaten teams in their respective groups. Twenty minutes each half.

The winning team will receive ten thousand ringgit for their school.

And then Nurhayati's dad drops his bombshell.

The best player of the final, as chosen by the headmasters of the two teams, will win a trip to England for the Brazil–England exhibition match at Wembley Stadium next month.

I can't believe it! A trip to England . . . to Wembley!

If *I* win . . .

I'll get to visit Foyles . . .

I'll watch Zico play live . . .

I'll get to see Dad!

CHAPTER
THIRTY-NINE

Rajiv, if I win, I'll get to see Dad!"

I'm so excited, I keep juggling the ball on the spot.

He looks at me and there are two frown lines between his eyes.

"You won't win."

"Why not? I'm the best player!"

"You won't win because it's a setup."

"What do you mean?"

"Nurhayati's dad is running for reelection. This is just a grand gesture to impress voters." He motions with his hands and I look around at the crowd.

"So? He deserves everyone's votes. If I was old enough, I'd vote for him!"

"The judges will give the tickets to Nurhayati. They know what's supposed to happen—he doesn't even have to tell them. That's why he's not one of the judges. It's politics. You'll understand when you're older."

"I *am* older!"

"Than me?"

He had me there. "Than I ever was before!"

Rajiv grabs me by the shoulders. The ball rolls away. Is that bad luck?

"Look at me, Maya!"

I reluctantly meet his gaze.

"I don't want you to be disappointed, that's all."

I swallow hard. It feels like I have a soccerball stuck in my throat. I can't speak. I nod to show that I understand, even though I don't really.

CHAPTER
FORTY

t's a close game.

We can't score because they have excellent defenders.

And I have to admit that I'm off my game. I've hit the side netting twice and the post and the crossbar once each. Normally, I'd have buried those chances. It's because of what Rajiv said. I can't get it out of my head.

Luckily, they can't score either, because their strikers are ordinary . . . and we have Batumalar.

At halftime the score is still 0–0.

Nurhayati's dad is worried. I can tell that he doesn't know what to do tactically. He's not a professional coach, after all.

He says, "It's up to you, Maya. You have to score if we're going to win this game."

Was that what the Brazil coach said to Zico just before he came on and missed that penalty?

Was that what my dad would have said if he was here,

watching the most important game of my life, instead of far away looking for his last chance at happiness?

"I believe in you." Nurhayati's dad puts his arm around my shoulders and gives me a quick hug as he says it.

To everyone's surprise including my own, I burst into tears. Just like that. I'm sobbing like Maradona after he won the World Cup. Except that I haven't won anything yet. And I won't win anything. Not this game, not the tickets, nothing.

The team gathers around close. They pat me on the back and murmur comforting words. I sob even louder. What's the matter with me?

"I'm sorry, Maya—I didn't mean to put you under so much pressure. It's just that you're our best player by miles."

That was it. I rounded on Nurhayati's dad as if he was a referee who'd just awarded an unjust penalty to the other side.

"You say—you say I'm the best player—but you're going to give those plane tickets to your own daughter. I know you are! It's not fair. I need those tickets!"

I almost blurt out that I need them so I can see Dad again but stop myself in time.

"I understand."

He smiles, but it's one of those twisty ones—just like Mom's. Maybe he feels guilty. But to be honest, he looks like he's really sad underneath. What kind of world do we live in when even the mayor can do only twisty smiles?

"Two minutes," says Batumalar.

Great. The second half is about to start, and we don't have a plan because I've been blubbering the whole time. I bet this never happens to Brazil.

"Maya, what number do you have on your back?" he asks.

"Ten."

Ten—just like Zico, Maradona, and Pelé.

A movie reel of soccer highlights plays in my head. Zico taking the second penalty after missing the first, Maradona's second goal against England, Pelé scoring in a World Cup when he was just seventeen.

Soccer is not just about skill; it's also about courage.

I look at Batumalar, Sok Mun, and even Nurhayati. In their own way, every single one of them has shown real guts to be here.

The other team runs onto the field for the second half. They look focused, determined, scary.

Do I have what it takes to be worthy of the shirt? Am I a number 10?

ajiv runs down to the field. He pats me on the back and sees my tears but doesn't say anything. It's just as well, or we might have been in for a second round of crying, and there's no time left.

He says, "Message from Mom . . ."

I look at him in surprise. What could Mom have to say about the game or our tactics or anything? She replaced herself with a rosebush when I was practicing. Maybe she just wants to wish me luck. That's very good of her, of course, but we need goals, not luck.

Rajiv says, "Mom says to remember that they're all just rosebushes."

I look at him and grin. I wipe the tears away with my sleeve.

They're all just rosebushes.

When the whistle blows for the start of the second half, I receive the ball and take them on.

I feint left and nutmeg the first defender. The ball rolls right between her legs.

For the second, I dip my left shoulder and go right. She's left standing.

Two more defenders come at me. I slow down as if I'm not sure what to do and then accelerate between them. They crash into each other behind me.

Their best defender is closing in. I shield the ball with my body. My back is to the goal. I roll the ball onto my foot, do my keepie-uppie thing for a couple of bounces, and then flick the ball over her head and mine. I swivel around and am past her with a clear shot at the goal.

The goalie looks terrified, but she comes out to narrow the angle.

I raise my foot as if I'm going to put every bit of strength I have into the shot. She flinches. I tuck the ball into the corner of the net: 1–0.

The crowd goes wild. I see Rajiv and Mom jump out of their seats in excitement.

I feel I've just scored the winning goal in the most important tournament of my life.

Maybe I have.

CHAPTER
FORTY-TWO

I t's "backs against the wall" time. The other team is pouring forward. They have no choice. The only thing between the two teams is my goal.

They seem stronger than us, and in better shape. Some of my teammates can barely run anymore. Nurhayati is just wandering around in a daze. Not even the presence of the boy she likes in the audience is enough to keep her going, she's that tired. I wonder how her dad can even consider letting her win the tickets, and then I put the thought out of my head. That's not important now.

Only Batumalar keeps us in the game. She is performing heroically. Tipping shots over the bar, pushing attempts onto the posts. Can she keep going?

I have given up trying to widen our lead or anything like that. I'm playing so deep in defense, I'm like an extra goalie, except that I can't use my hands.

Their best striker gets the ball.

She's running toward our goal.

Nurhayati sticks out a leg and the striker skips over it.

She hits a thunderous shot.

Batumalar just manages to get a hand on it.

The ball rebounds into play.

The striker and I lunge for the ball.

She gets there first.

I get there second.

She gets the ball.

I get the player.

It's a penalty.

CHAPTER
FORTY-THREE

I can hardly believe what I've done. There are only two minutes left in the game.

Two minutes!

What was I thinking?

I should have realized I couldn't get to the ball in time and concentrated on staying goal-side of the striker. I'd have narrowed her angle for the shot and Batumalar would have done the rest.

I've just conceded a penalty *two* minutes before the end of the game.

And for once it's not happening in my head.

This is not me pretending to be Zico.

This is not me imagining myself on the pitch in the middle of the night while watching television.

This is not me practicing in the yard.

It's real. This is *me* losing the game for my team in front of family and friends and crowds of people. Complete strangers know how badly I've messed up.

For the first time, I'm glad Dad is not in the audience.

I'm also glad I don't have a real chance to win that ticket to England because of politics or whatever. If I *had* a real chance, I just lost it, and that would be too hard to bear.

If I'd stayed on my feet, I might have deserved to see Dad, Zico, and Foyles in the same week. But not now.

Now I'm going to have to wear a bag over my head to avoid being recognized around Kuantan.

Their striker is placing the ball.

Batumalar is swinging her arms in a windmill, keeping herself loose. I shake my head in admiration. She's a real pro.

A hockey goal isn't that big, but Batumalar is only eleven. There seems to be a lot of space for a talented striker to slip the ball past her.

The striker is three yards behind the ball. She's planning a long run-up. That probably means she's going for power. If she gets the ball on target, there won't be much poor Batumalar can do about it.

Nurhayati wanders over and claps me on the back.

"It wasn't your fault, Maya. You were just unlucky."

My heart feels like warm toast. The team is sticking by me. I don't deserve it, but it feels good.

It happens in a flash.

The other team's striker goes for power and placement. It's

an amazing shot, flying like an arrow into the top right-hand corner.

Time slows down.

I remember Platini missing his penalty against Brazil.

I remember Germany tying the score from two down in the final.

I remember Burruchaga winning the World Cup for Argentina.

I swear that none of those moments compares to Batumalar getting her fingertips to the ball and tipping it over the bar.

As we jump up and down in excitement, hug each other, and run to Batumalar to hug her, I hear the crowd. They are chanting "Batumalar, Batumalar."

I know in that instant that Sister Pauline will never make Batumalar do squats again.

CHAPTER
FORTY-FOUR

Nurhayati's dad is not our coach anymore. He's the main dignitary, sitting in an armchair under a striped awning. In Malaysia, the most important person always sits in an armchair that looks as if it's been brought in from someone's home. He is flanked by various school reps, but they have only plastic chairs to indicate their lesser importance.

The announcer invites him to present the medals. It takes ages because there are participation medals, bronze medals, and silver medals to get through first.

I don't mind. I'm savoring every minute.

Finally, it's our turn.

Each girl gets a *gold* medal.

As the captain, I get to hold the trophy aloft. I don't cry— I'm not Maradona and I used up my tears earlier anyway—but I am the proudest I have ever been.

Our headmaster, Mr. de Cruz, receives the outsize mock

check for ten thousand ringgit, and he's grinning like the Cheshire Cat. Maybe next time he won't ask me whether money grows on trees when we need uniforms.

And then Nurhayati's dad takes the mike.

He says, "The time has come to name the Player of the Final. The winner and an accompanying adult will, as promised, be flown to England to attend the Brazil–England friendly to be played at Wembley Stadium next month. The choice was made by the two heads of the schools participating in the final."

We are all watching him.

I know Nurhayati will get it.

I know there is no hope, but I can't help hoping.

Then I remember that I conceded the penalty. Batumalar deserves it more than I do anyway for saving the shot.

Or they might feel they need to give the runners-up something to cheer about, in which case they'll probably hand it to that big striker from Beserah who missed the penalty.

I look across at her. She's crying. It's not much use being the best player on your team and a contender for Player of the Final if you missed the penalty that would have kept your team in the match.

Soccer can be a cruel game.

Just ask Zico.

"It was a much harder decision to make than anyone expected," continues Nurhayati's dad.

Despite everything, I want to believe that a man who understands the value of a number-10 jersey cannot be a cheat.

"Nurhayati, who also happens to be my daughter, played with real courage."

The disappointment is like a high tackle to the gut. I feel winded. He's going to give the ticket to see Zico, *my* Zico, to his own kid. It's not fair.

"But Batumalar, a last-minute substitute when the regular goalkeeper was injured, put in an immense effort . . . including saving a penalty!"

I cheer and clap. She deserves to win. And at least Nurhayati's dad hasn't let me down. I am horribly disappointed to miss out on seeing Dad, but the judges don't know that I have a special reason for wanting to go to England.

He turns to look at me.

The two judges, Mr. de Cruz and the headmistress from the other school, are looking at me as well.

Do I have mud on my nose?

They're all smiling.

But they're twisty smiles.

I realize in that moment that everyone already knows that Dad has left Mom and Rajiv and me to live in England. My big secret is no secret at all.

"But for an overall performance worthy of the number-10 jersey and for scoring the winning goal in the final, the ticket to England goes to Maya 'Zico' David!"

This time I bawl like Maradona.

Nurhayati's dad hugs me.

Mom and Rajiv hug me.

Soon, Dad will get a chance to hug me too.

CHAPTER
FORTY-FIVE

don't want to tell Dad I'm coming. I want it to be a surprise.
A *big* surprise.

Mom's not sure about this.

"I don't think it's a good idea, Maya, to not tell your father
you're coming."

"It will be such a great surprise, Mom."

She looks doubtful and I know her head is full of visions of
Dad breaking my heart by not being happy to see me.

I can't explain to Mom, of course, but the thing is I'm not
sure I *could* be more hurt than I am now. I have such a sore
place in my heart because Dad missed seeing my winning goal.
Because of the twisty smiles from everyone around me, even
Nurhayati's dad. And because Rajiv is working so hard to be the
man of the house and he's only a skinny teenager.

And if I tell Dad I'm going to England, he'll have plenty

of time to think of good reasons why he can't come back to Kuantan and be our dad again.

I know what grownups are like. They hate admitting they've made a mistake.

And the bigger the mistake, the less they like admitting they were wrong.

Besides, I have a plan. And I can't tell Mom or Rajiv what it is because I'm pretty sure they're not going to like it.

So it really has to be a surprise.

CHAPTER
FORTY-SIX

Time flies when you're about to see your dad. In no time at all Mom and I are on a big Boeing 747 to London.

Amamma is staying at home to keep an eye on Rajiv. Poor Rajiv.

He's being very decent about it. I know he wishes he could come and see Dad too, but he's too young to be my "accompanying adult." That's what Nurhayati's dad says, anyway, and he tends to know about this sort of thing.

I would love to tell Rajiv about my plan to get Dad back so that he doesn't have to feel sad about missing out on this trip. But I'm afraid he won't think it's a good idea and might feel that he has to be all grown-up and responsible and tell Mom what I'm planning to do.

Or, even if he doesn't stop me, he might tell me that it won't work and I'm just going to make a fool of myself. He may be right, of course. In fact, he's probably right.

But I know he wants Dad to come home just as much as I do. I want to get Dad back for *both* of us.

I'm not dumb enough to believe my plan is sure to work.

But if there's one thing I've learned from soccer, it's that every obstacle in life is a rosebush. Including anything standing in the way of your dad coming home.

I say to Rajiv as firmly as I can, "Just make sure you watch the game on television."

"It's only an exhibition," he grumbles. "And you know I don't like soccer that much."

I shake my head and juggle a ball on my knee.

"You've *got* to watch, Rajiv. You might spot me in the crowd."

Rajiv smiles. "There'll be thousands of people at Wembley!"

I am getting desperate. "Please, Rajiv. Promise you'll watch?"

He laughs and puts an arm around my shoulder. "All right, I will."

I wonder whether Rajiv will go on being a great brother when Dad comes home or whether he'll be a pain again when he's not the man of the house anymore. I hope he doesn't go back to being the sort of brother who would support Germany in a World Cup final. But it's a risk I have to take. We need a dad.

CHAPTER
FORTY-SEVEN

om wants to call Dad when we arrive in London, but I refuse.

"The game's tomorrow, Mom. Let's just wait."

"But you've been so anxious to see your father again . . ."

Mom is really puzzled.

"But I want to see Zico first, Mom!"

The next day, I'm up at dawn. I'm so excited. This is going to be the best day of my life.

Mom has carefully washed and ironed my uniform. I plan to wear the blue shorts and yellow number-10 shirt to the match. I don't want anyone to think I am supporting England!

When I get dressed, I slip on an extra layer under my jersey. It's all part of my brilliant plan to get Dad back.

If things work out the way they're supposed to, he won't be able to turn me down. I just know he won't.

A small voice in my head says, "What if things don't work out the way they're supposed to?" I try to ignore it but it's persistent—like a coach trying to drum some positional sense into Brazilian defenders before a World Cup knockout round.

I put my hands over my ears, but that doesn't shut out the voice in my head.

What if things *don't* work out the way they're supposed to?

CHAPTER
FORTY-EIGHT

ho would ever have thought that the first time I visited a stadium it would be Wembley?

Wembley!

Pelé calls Wembley the cathedral of soccer.

The two big towers are so much more imposing in real life than on TV.

The crowds of people streaming in are laughing and shouting and singing. Mom clutches my hand tight and looks nervous because these are real-life rowdy English fans with beer guts and tattoos, shaved heads, and painted faces. But I'm not worried. They just love their soccer and their team. I know the feeling well. I may be scrawny and brown and wearing Brazil colors—but under my skin I'm just like them.

Besides, Mom doesn't know it, but she has a lot more to worry about than hooligans.

Walking through the spectator tunnels and seeing the perfect green grass for the first time is *magic*.

The field is much bigger than I imagined.

I can't *wait* to turn professional and play here myself. Even Amamma might think that girls should be allowed to play soccer if she could see Wembley.

There are players warming up. I spot Branco and Sócrates, but Zico is not out yet.

I realize that he might not start the game.

They'd better bring him on as a substitute. I haven't come all the way to England to watch Brazil play and have Zico sit on the bench for the whole game.

The players go back into the tunnel.

I look around. There must be seventy-five thousand people packed into the stadium. Most of them are in white, but there are large pockets of yellow scattered about—my fellow supporters of Brazil dancing the samba.

Our seats are quite a long way up—on the third tier. But they are on the aisle. I make Mom sit on the inside. Vendors carry trays of junk food and drinks and I ask Mom if I can have some fries. She agrees and gives me money, and I hurry down toward the vendor. There is another one much closer, but I pretend not to notice. I need to see the layout farther down.

The field is separated from the spectators by a low barrier. I lean on the barrier, and a policeman in a silly hat—a bobby

—glares at me. I smile at him but then scurry back to my seat.

There's no reason to get into trouble *before* it's time to get into trouble.

The match is about to begin. I am bouncing up and down in my seat. Even Mom is excited. Her hair is windblown and her smile is happy, not twisty at all.

The players run out one by one, and the crowd—including me—goes wild as the names are announced over the loudspeakers. So many of my heroes are in the starting lineup—Sócrates, Falcão, Branco, and Careca.

But not Zico. He's on the bench.

The game is electrifying.

Usually, on TV, you just get to see the man on the ball. There is no perspective on the rest of the team taking up positions or running into space. Not even when they make darting runs into the penalty box, track back after a forward run, or sprint down the wing to cross the ball to the middle. And it's strange not to have the instant replay on television.

I wonder for a second if I will ever be able to watch soccer on TV again. It is just so fantastic in real life.

Unfortunately, being eleven years old, I miss a lot when the people in front of me leap to their feet in excitement. I'm too short to see anything when they do that. I decide to jump on my seat the minute the ball gets into the last third. Otherwise, I might miss a goal.

I miss a goal.

In my hurry to get on my chair, I slip, and by the time I make it into my seat, Sócrates has curled one in.

I *do* see England's goal to tie the game. I'd have been quite happy to miss Lineker scramble the ball over the line. Typical Brazilian mix-up between goalie and last defender. Some things never change.

At halftime the score is 1–1.

Mom asks me if I would like a drink or a hot dog, but I shake my head. My insides are all churned up like the six-yard box on a rainy day.

I decide that the sixtieth minute is when I will execute my plan to get Dad back.

Time is moving slowly. I watch the clock more than the game.

In the fiftieth minute there is a huge roar from the crowd, even the England fans.

I stare at the field, wondering what I've missed.

Then I see the fourth official holding up the board to announce a substitution for Brazil.

Number 10 is coming in.

Zico is coming in!

I feel lucky.

The game finally enters the sixtieth minute.

CHAPTER
FORTY-NINE

I look at Mom.

I feel a moment of doubt.

What if this is a horribly bad idea?

What if my plan doesn't work?

What if I'm arrested and spend the rest of my life in a tiny cell without a soccerball?

There's only one way to find out. I'm not going to die wondering, that's for sure.

I lean over, put an arm around Mom, and give her a quick hug.

She turns to me in surprise.

I grin, get to my feet, and skip down the steps until I'm leaning on the barrier by the field.

I wait until the bobby is facing the other way.

Then I scramble over the railing.

A ball boy is looking at me, his mouth hanging open.

All the people in the stadium, all seventy-five thousand, are watching the game.

There's only a narrow strip of ground between the field and me.

I am close to the center circle.

I take a deep breath, think of Dad, think of Dad coming home, think of Rajiv's face when he sees me on TV, and dash onto the field.

CHAPTER
FIFTY

I run as fast as I can.

At first, no one notices. Falcao thunders past me. He slides a pass to Júlio César, who has made a run down the wing.

And then Glenn Hoddle spots me.

He realizes that the small figure in Brazil colors is not an underfed Brazilian substitute.

They've all stopped playing now.

I am still running for the center circle. The pitch is *huge* when you're just eleven years old.

The crowd, which fell silent when the game ground to a standstill, is yelling and cheering now.

There's nothing soccer spectators like more than a field invasion.

A field invasion is not half as much fun on TV because they point the cameras somewhere else so as not to "encourage" such behavior. Usually, it's streakers who run on—buck-naked and very, very drunk. I considered being naked, but in the end I decided that it would probably be the death of Amamma. Also, I need this to be on television or there's no point.

In any event, no one has seen an eleven-year-old from Kuantan heading for the center circle at Wembley before, so I'm enough of a surprise to keep the crowd's attention.

I see Zico out of the corner of my eye.

He has the ball under his arm and is jogging slowly toward me, a confused expression on his face. He's even better looking in real life. Maybe he thinks I'm the Brazil mascot and I'm just lost.

I reach the center circle.

I rip off my yellow jersey.

Underneath is the white T-shirt I painted the week before we left.

I am in the middle of the pitch at Wembley Stadium in the sixtieth minute of a match between Brazil and England.

The score is 1–1 and the players are almost upon me.

All of them, including Zico and the referee and the linesmen and the people in the stands and the TV cameras, can see my T-shirt with the words in big, bold letters: DAD, PLEASE COME HOME!

CHAPTER
FIFTY-ONE

My plea doesn't work.

Dad won't come home.

I am a nine days' wonder—the kid who wanted her dad to come back so badly that she was prepared to announce it at Wembley in the middle of a soccer game.

But Dad won't come home.

My pitch invasion is in the newspapers and on television.

Zico holds a press conference and says that family is very important to him and gives me a number-10 Brazil shirt signed by the whole team.

But Dad won't come home.

"Why not?" I demand.

"I didn't leave because of you or Rajiv, so I can't come home because of the two of you."

"But you didn't see my winning goal! And Rajiv is the only one without a dad at his hockey matches."

"It didn't stop you from scoring the goal, did it? And Rajiv is still playing hockey, right?"

"It's not the same."

He sighs and tries to take my hand, but I back away and put my arms behind my back. I know I'm being childish and I can see the hurt in Dad's eyes, but it makes me feel happy in a mean kind of way. If he won't come back, he needs to understand how it feels when your own family lets you down.

"That was some stunt you pulled," he says.

"I know." I can't help feeling proud, even though it hasn't worked. Imagine, me invading the field at Wembley!

"You could have just asked me to come home."

"You hardly ever call anymore."

"That's because neither of you seems to want to speak to me." His voice cracks, but I refuse to feel sorry for him.

"We want to speak to you in person!"

"I'm not sure a T-shirt at Wembley is speaking to me in person."

Fair point. "I guess not."

"Then why did you do it?"

"I wanted to ask you to come home in a way that you couldn't ignore."

"Even though you knew it wouldn't work?"

"I didn't know that!"

I'm yelling, but the voice in my head is busy saying *I told you so.*

Deep down, I always knew it wasn't going to work.

So why did I do it?

I look at Dad and he looks at me. He's just the same really, a bit less tubby around the tummy—not enough Indian food probably—a can of cola in his right hand, his glasses perched on the end of his nose.

"I guess I wanted you to feel ashamed for leaving Rajiv and me like that."

"In which case I think we can call Operation Wembley a success." He smiles as he says it. It seems that he hasn't forgotten how to do a twisty smile, even though he's been gone for so long.

"But you won't come back?"

"No. But that doesn't mean I don't love you and Rajiv as much as I always did and always will." He sighs. "It's just that life doesn't always turn out exactly the way we want it."

I sigh. That's something I understand all too well.

If life turned out exactly the way I wanted it, then Zico wouldn't have missed that penalty. But if Brazil had beaten France and reached the final, Germany would probably have won the World Cup again. And Maradona might not have scored that wonder goal against England.

So if I get everything I want, it means someone else has to be unhappy.

Like Dad. Or Mom. Or Maradona.

Frankly, that's too much responsibility for an eleven-year-old, even one with a shirt signed by the whole Brazil team.

Maybe I should have painted ZICO, WILL YOU MARRY ME? on my T-shirt instead.

Dad holds out his hand again, and this time I grab it.

He takes me to Foyles. It's even more magical than I could have imagined. He buys me all the books I want and promises to call more often and visit Kuantan once in a while, now that his job is going pretty well and he's saving some money. He says he was sorry to have missed my tournament and especially my winning goal, but that he's as proud of me as if he'd been there.

And then we go for lunch and he introduces me to a friend of his, a white lady, and at first I don't know what it means, but then I see them holding hands.

She has a daughter about my age, who sticks out her tongue at me when no one is watching. She's picking on the wrong kid. I've been fouled enough on the field when the referee was looking the other way not to care about insults that don't leave bruises.

"Do you play soccer?" I ask.

"Of course not; that's a boys' game. I take ballet."

I imagine Dad at a ballet recital, longing for a glass of cider, and I snort so loud that orange juice comes out of my nose.

"What's the matter, honey?" Dad asks.

"Nothing," I say. "Nothing at all."

CHAPTER
FIFTY-TWO

In a few days I am on a plane home with Mom, who has not spoken to me since Wembley.

We reach the Kuantan airport and walk slowly through the arrival hall. London was cool with Big Ben and Tower Bridge and Buckingham Palace, but it feels good to be home.

I spot Nurhayati and wonder what she is doing at the airport. Setting off on another expensive holiday, probably. And then I see Batumalar and Sok Mun and Nurhayati's dad and Batumalar's too and Mr. de Cruz, the headmaster, and the rest of my team, and Rajiv, and Amamma.

Amamma!

They are holding a banner that reads WELCOME HOME, MAYA "ZICO" DAVID! It is like winning the World Cup, and I cry and hug everyone as tightly as I can and they hug me back even harder than when I scored the winning goal in the final of our tournament.

I whisper to Rajiv, "Dad wouldn't come home. Even after what I did."

He nods and shrugs. "I like being man of the house anyway."

I know he is lying. We both smile twisty smiles.

I guess things don't always work out the way we'd like.

But I still have Rajiv and Mom and lots of friends and a number-10 Brazil shirt signed by Zico and the rest of the team. I've finally been to Foyles, and when I'm a grown-up professional soccer player, I'll probably see more of Dad. Maybe even sooner when he gets tired of Miss Ballet Shoes.

Amamma, who has been hanging back, comes forward now. She looks tiny wrapped in her all-white sari, and I remember that she claims she is not long for this world. For the first time, I believe her. After a week of not having her loom large in my imagination, I see how small and frail she is.

Impulsively, I hug her.

If there's one thing I've learned, it's the importance of family.

"I'm sorry I embarrassed you in London, Amamma. I know that invading the field at Wembley wasn't right for a well-behaved Indian girl."

A tear runs down her cheek. It follows a slow path, along the wrinkle lines, until it reaches her chin. It hovers there for a moment like a referee's hand over his breast pocket as he decides whether to hand out a yellow or red card.

"You are like your mother—headstrong and foolish."

I nod.

"She would not listen when I told her that no good would come of marrying your father."

I nod again.

"So you too will make many mistakes."

"Yes, Amamma."

"You and your brother will embarrass me often, so I have nowhere to hide my face in the whole *country*."

I catch Rajiv's eye. His nose is a previously unseen color—bluish. What does that mean?

I consider promising not to do anything to upset her again and then decide against it. I would just end up breaking my word, and that's not a good thing. I'm definitely going to fail Amamma's behavior tests at some point.

"But you are still my much-loved grandchildren, even though you are too thin and too tall, and that will not change."

I stare at her and then at Mom and Rajiv. We're all gaping at one another as we contemplate what Amamma has just said.

Much-loved grandchildren?

I poke a finger in my ear and dig around in case the wax has made me deaf.

"Unless, of course, you bring *real* shame upon the family."

"How would we do that?" asks Rajiv.

I see what he means. What could be worse than a televised field invasion to demand the return of a runaway white dad?

"If you *also* marry the wrong person—like your mother."

"Blimey!" (That's a word I learned in England.)

Rajiv, Mom, and I exchange smiles, and they're not twisty smiles this time. And then we start to laugh and laugh until our sides hurt and we're bent over double, clutching our tummies.

I wonder whether to tell Amamma I still plan to marry Zico. Would she consider him a "wrong person"? Or does she understand now that magic feet are more important than any skin color?

Better find out another day, I decide.

In the meantime, I saw a neat trick by Careca—a triple step over—and I can't wait to try it in the yard.

"Ready to go, Maya?"

"Yes, Mom. Let's go home!"

A Note from the Author

Hi, Readers,

The soccer World Cup I write about in *Ten* was held in Mexico in 1986. If you like, you can look up the games on YouTube and watch Zico miss the penalty in the quarterfinal against France, Maradona's two amazing goals against England, and the fabulous final between Germany and Argentina.

The Wembley Stadium I describe in the book has been torn down. A new, modern stadium has been built in its place. I loved the old stadium with its two tower blocks because that's where I saw Brazil play for the first time (an exhibition against England). Brazil won 3–1.

When my daughter, Sasha (short for Alexandra and named after Alex Ferguson, the Manchester United manager for many years), turned thirteen, she had a wicked left foot and a sharp eye for the goal. Unfortunately, in Malaysia, there are still not many girl players, so she played on an all boys' team in an all boys' league, which, she assured me, was quite awful a lot of the time! She hopes to come to the United States to play someday.

Sasha asked me recently, "Is *Ten* a true story?"

It's a difficult question to answer.

Many things in the book are true, but eleven-year-old me never played soccer or scored a winning goal (or any other sort of goal for that matter). But I did long to do so from the very first moment I watched a soccer game on a black-and-white television in the middle of the night while my parents yelled at each other upstairs.

In fact, I began this book because my childhood didn't have a happy ending, and I wanted to write one for myself. By the time I finished writing it, I knew that I didn't need to make up a happy ending. I might not have had a perfect childhood, but who does? My dad might not have come home, but I'm not the only child in the world who didn't have a dad around much while growing up. I realized as I wrote this book that life is about making the best of things.

After all, I never played soccer as a child, but I do now as an adult. I still watch the game on television, I've written this book about my favorite sport, *and* I've taught my daughter a real love of the beautiful game. Who knows, maybe she'll score the winner in a World Cup final someday!

I call that a happy ending and I hope you do too.

Shamini Flint

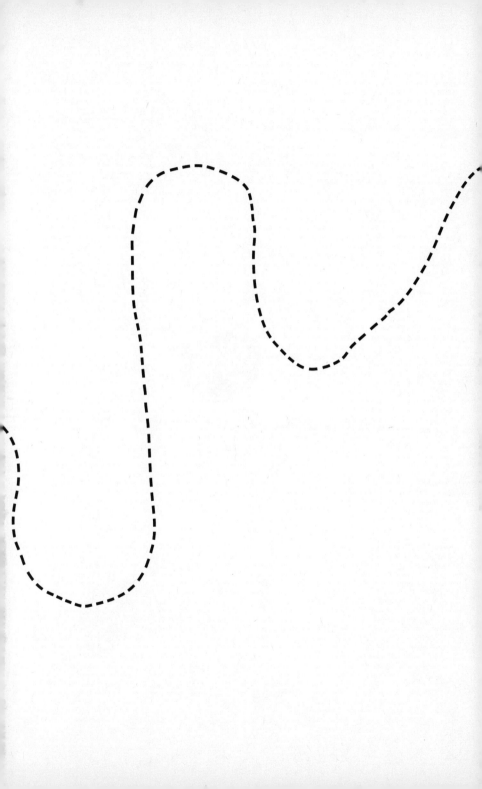